Books in

The Human-Hybrid Project

series:

TheGlass
Siege

TheGlass Siege

Farley L. Dunn

THREE SKILLET

Published in Fort Worth, Texas

 THREE SKILLET

www.ThreeSkilletPublishing.com

Three Skillet Publishing
PO Box 162194
Fort Worth, Texas 76161

ISBN: 978-1-943189-98-4

Printed in the USA

TheGlass Siege

— Book 5 —

The Human-Hybrid Project

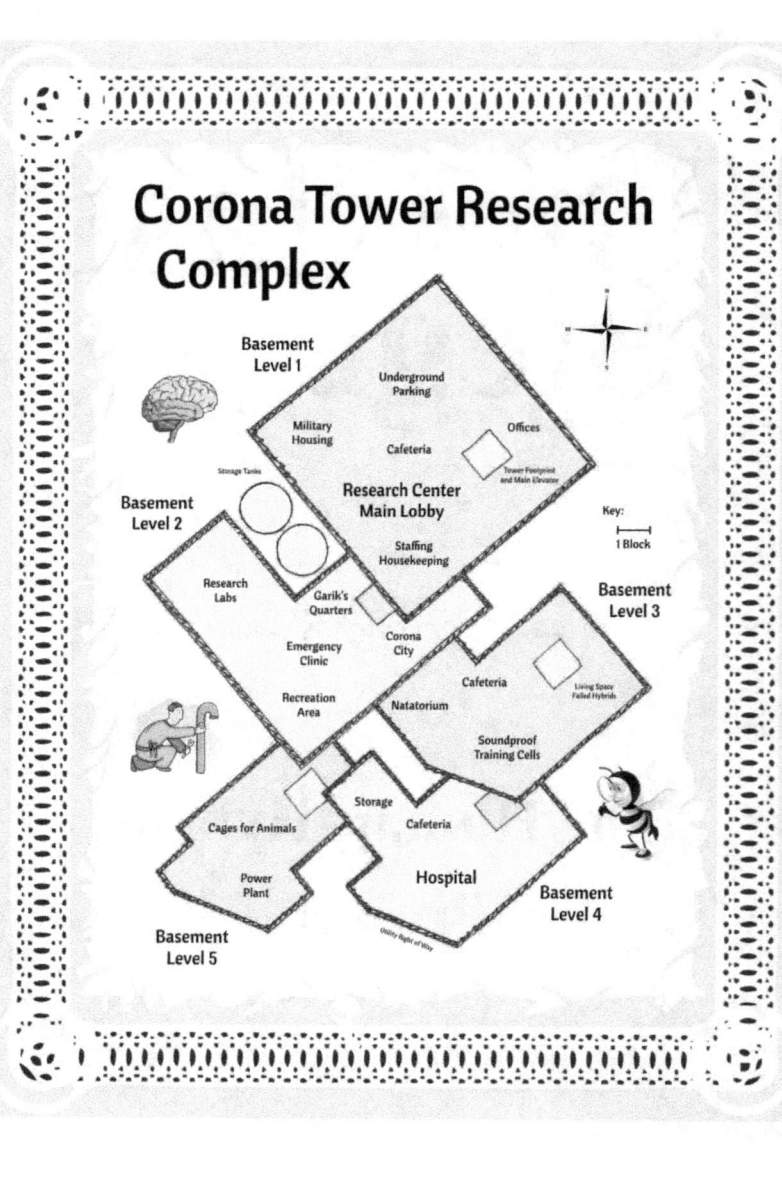

Corona Tower Research Complex

Basement Level 1

Underground Parking

Military Housing

Cafeteria

Offices

Storage Tanks

Research Center Main Lobby

Tower Footprint and Main Elevator

Basement Level 2

Staffing Housekeeping

Research Labs

Garik's Quarters

Corona City

Emergency Clinic

Cafeteria

Basement Level 3

Living Space Failed Hybrids

Recreation Area

Natatorium

Soundproof Training Cells

Storage

Cages for Animals

Cafeteria

Power Plant

Hospital

Basement Level 4

Utility Right of Way

Basement Level 5

Key:
1 Block

Bay City
Uptown East Side

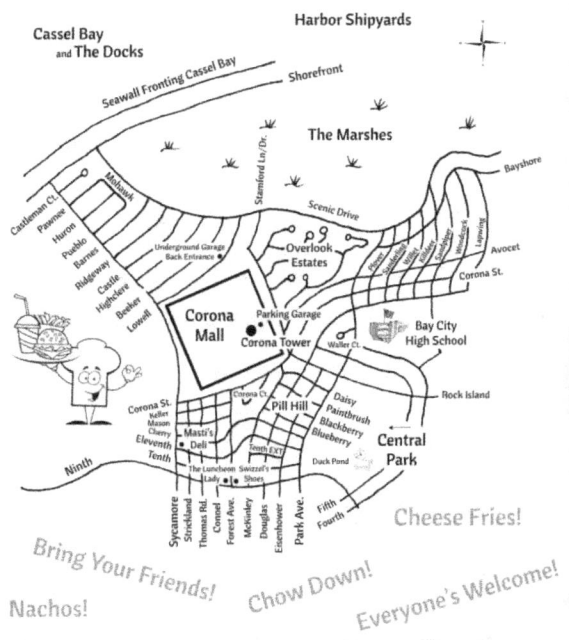

Cassel Bay
and The Docks

Harbor Shipyards

Seawall Fronting Cassel Bay

Shorefront

The Marshes

Scenic Drive

Bayshore

Castleman Ct.
Pawnee
Huron
Pueblo
Barnes
Ridgeway
Castle
Highclere
Beeker
Lovell

Stamford Ln./Dr.

Underground Garage
Back Entrance

Overlook
Estates

Avocet

Corona St.

Corona
Mall

Parking Garage
Corona Tower

Waller Ct.

Bay City
High School

Corona Ct.

Pill Hill

Daisy
Paintbrush
Blackberry
Blueberry

Rock Island

Corona St.
Keller
Mason
Cherry
Eleventh
Tenth

Masti's
Deli

Tenth EXT

Duck Pond

Central
Park

Ninth

The Luncheon
Lady

Swizzel's
Shoes

Sycamore
Strickland
Thomas Rd.
Conrad
Forest Ave.
McKinley
Douglas
Eisenhower
Park Ave.
Fifth
Fourth

Cheese Fries!

Bring Your Friends!

Chow Down!

Everyone's Welcome!

Nachos!

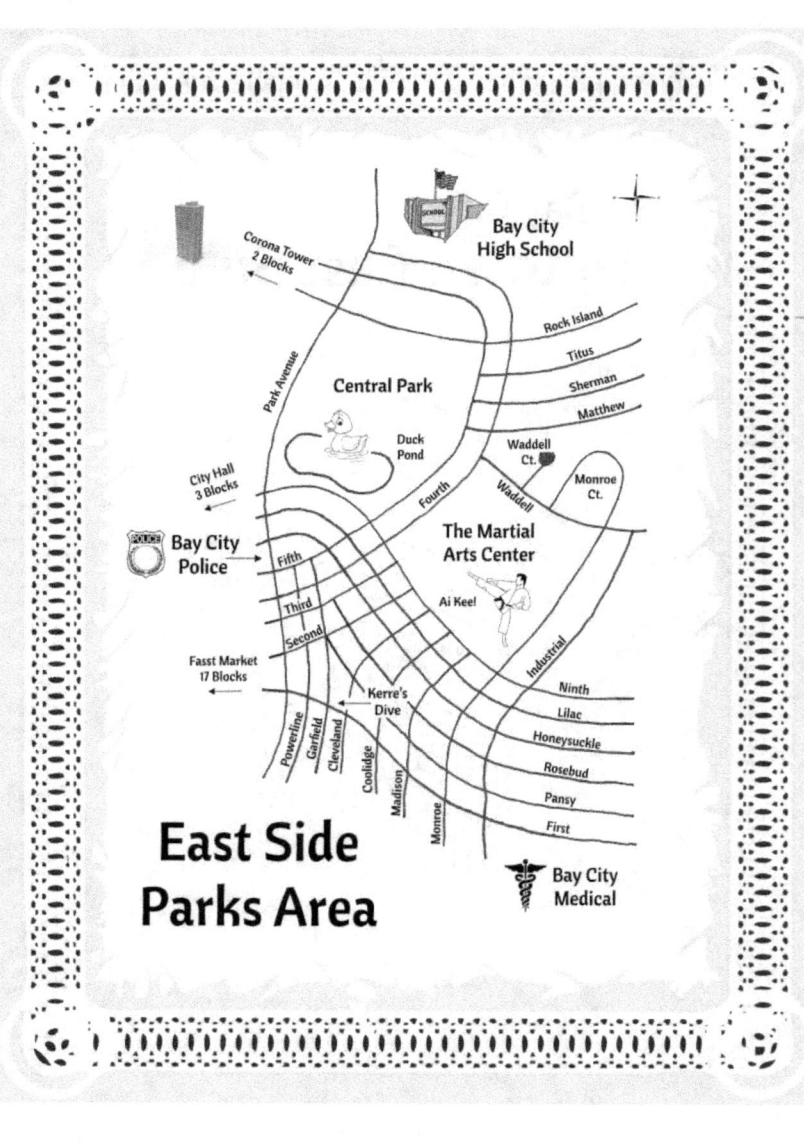

East Side
Parks Area

Bay City
Old Town East Side

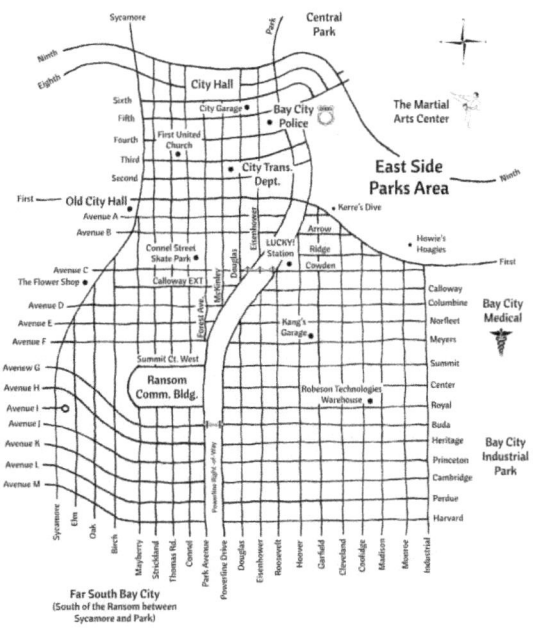

arik Shayk opened his eyes, unsure what had awakened him. The soft murmur of air moving through the grille high in the wall overhead lulled him into a pleasant memory: his girlfriend, Marisa Bruni, and sitting together under the stars on the rooftop of their apartment building; the drawing she had created for him on her Micro-Art tablet of an electrified sword; the mesmerizing hold her face had on him.

The memory was shattered by the percussive sounds of the Howling Pterodactyls, the eponymous Rez band of all Rez bands, in concert at the Corona

Mall. The driving beat grew louder, and he looked around the room. A glow from under a closed door revealed various pieces of furniture and several additional openings, one showing the brighter gleam of porcelain fixtures. Another one, open and dark, likely a closet.

The driving beat of the Dactyls became a hammer on metal.

"Ah, Arik!" Garik came fully awake with a rush of anger. Arik Oblonsky was his aunt Irina's deadbeat boyfriend, and it was like him to intentionally get on Garik's nerves. He tossed his bedding aside and forced himself to restrain his rising irritation, reminding himself, "Anger gets me nothing. Arik wins if I react. My hands, my mind, the only way." He must be in control of his feelings, or his world would quickly spiral out of his control.

He laid back the door, only to be reminded he wasn't in his aunt's apartment in Bay City any longer. Devon Maye, the activities coordinator for the underground and very secretive human-hybrid project, stood in the small kitchen, *Garik's small kitchen*, in the underground research center under Corona Mall WHERE GARIK HAD BEEN HIJACKED AND IMPRISONED. Joseph Howard and Tyrone Brown, Tower workers he recognized, were head-to-head at the front door, deep in conversation. Garik's memories of Marisa and their time under the stars evaporated, no more than a teasing soap bubble, bright and shiny, and effervescently temporary.

"Right-o, kiddo, about time to wake those sleepy eyes." Devon, physically fit with blond hair and a trademark cowlick at his temple, opened a cupboard door and lifted out two plates. "I've got work today, and you're with me."

"With you?" Garik rubbed his face. "Remind me why you're in my apartment."

"Still doing that, are you? Repeating people?" Devon spooned a pile of eggs onto each plate. From the toaster oven, he pulled out four buttered muffins and nearly dropped one when it was hotter than he expected. "Ouch, ouch. Get it while it's hot."

"Okay." Garik took one of the plates and a fork and found the couch. "I remember you here last night. Refresh my memory."

"I am officially your babysitter." Devon joined him at the opposite end of the couch with a plate of his own. Folded bedding served as his end table. He began to fork in his breakfast.

"Oh, yeah." With the word *babysitter*, Garik's one night of freedom from the secretive basement research complex underneath the forty-story Corona Tower glass skyscraper unfolded before him. Months before, his life had been usurped when he was forcibly inducted into the human-hybrid project and injected with timber wolf DNA in the hope that he would mutate into a military tool with precog abilities. Jantzen Hefferly, able to morph into a cloud of purple mist, had enabled Garik and twelve other human hybrids to escape the Tower's clutches. Foolishly—although he hadn't thought so at the time—Garik had tried to reconnect with his girlfriend, Marisa, and had gotten himself recaptured. Now, weeks of planning were lost, and as a final insult, the previous evening, he had watched a woman be sucked into a bolt of supercharged lightning discharged by the tip of Halo Sunchaser's electrified sword. Weston Rodheimer bleeding electricity from his fingertips to charge the sword with crackling energy, then the glowing weapon eating the woman molecule by molecule, atom by atom, electron by electron, sucked away Garik's appetite like a whirlpool in a bottomless pit, and he set his plate on the floor, no longer interested.

"Eat up, kiddo. We've got a busy day." Devon had polished his plate, and he called to the workers at the door, "Joseph, Tyrone, I've got more if you're hungry."

Garik glanced their direction. Joseph and Tyrone were with maintenance and had installed Garik's ZBoard motorized skateboard charging station in his original quarters and later moved it to this one. It was still there, off to one side, blinking, telling him it was fully charged and ready to ride.

"Already eaten, but thanks. This door, don't think it's getting fixed today or tomorrow, likely. Custom build, need to order in panels to skin the damage. We'll be taking it away."

"How will we have any privacy?" Devon lifted one eyebrow.

We? Garik sagged. The truth of his situation hit him like a jackhammer. Devon's bed was Garik's couch. Devon had said babysitter but jailer was closer to the truth. And the damaged door, something else that was Garik's responsibility, a knife into his morning. Alyna Lindberg, DNA-enhanced with a Komodo dragon, had used her retractable claws to override the locking mechanism by slicing the door to shreds.

Devon stood, his plate empty, and took in Garik's uneaten food. He tapped the plate with the toe of one shoe. "Eat up, kiddo. Gonna be mighty hungry by lunch."

"Yah," Garik muttered, trying to push away the image of the girl that had gotten eaten by the electrified sword. His stomach was upside down.

"Seriously, you're mine, now, and I need to get out of here. Scoot, scoot."

"Yah, yah."

"And some clothes, kiddo. You chewed on me last night. I'm chewing on you, now." Devon was in the small kitchen, and he dropped his plate in the sink and flipped on the water.

Garik snorted, but the man was right. He needed to dress, and he stood, set the plate uneaten on the counter, and made his way to the bathroom. He leaned into the mirror, looking into his eyes. His friend, Muhammad Saud, had said his eyes were different. How? He couldn't find it. And the rest of him. No extra-long canines. No fur sprouting along his backbone. Even his hair. It was starting to curl again, and he had missed that. He was becoming the old Garik, lean and tight, if a bit bulkier from his training. That was a good thing, and he didn't mind that at all.

He yelled to Devon, "What are we doing this morning? I need to know what to wear."

"Training. It's what I do. Have you forgotten?"

"I don't follow you around all day." Sheesh! What did the man expect, for him to memorize his daily schedule?

"You are today." Devon leaned around the door frame from the living room, and he shook his head. He turned away, muttering, "It must be a teen thing."

"What?" How had he screwed up this time?

"You weren't supposed to hear that." Devon had his wrist up, his watch exposed, and he was prepared to tap the face with one finger.

"I can't help it you talk so loud. What's a teen thing? And what's wrong with being a teen? Am I supposed to act like an old man like you?"

"Hey!" Devon stepped into the bedroom. "That's unfair. You admiring yourself in the mirror all the time. Put on a shirt and comfortable shoes. I'm trying to get you new quarters, someplace with a real door. I want you ready when I'm off the phone."

Devon tapped his watch as he disappeared back to the main part of the apartment. "Lt. Shoate, please."

"Why not your place, then," Garik began to rant to himself, as he entered the closet and began pulling clothes off the racks and yanking them on. "Yah, Mr. Recreation Coordinator, or is your place too good for the hybrid wolf boy? You can come here, but I can't go there. Is that how it is? I've lived that life, don't like it, don't want to do it anymore. Sheesh! Quit treating me like a little boy—"

Garik dropped onto his bed to put on his shoes and looked up to Devon standing in the door with his arms crossed.

"I'll quit treating you like a boy when you quit acting like one."

"Yah, blame your life on me." Garik's anger boiled.

Still, the man's words hit home, and equally fast, remorse washed over him. He looked away and blinked his eyes to clear them. Yesterday morning he had been free, wandering the city, looking forward to meeting Marisa, telling her how much he had missed her. And now, now, this!

"Wasn't trying to."

Garik looked up and studied the man's face, trying to find someone he could trust in his eyes.

"My apologies for pushing you. Remember last night? Me on your couch? Not fun. Now, no door. Less fun. That's what I was on the phone about."

"The door's getting fixed?"

"Better, kiddo." Devon grinned. "We normal people can hear, too. Lt. Shoate better than most, and she liked your idea."

"My idea?" My idea? Yikes, doing it again, repeating other people's words, but Devon didn't seem to notice, for which he was grateful.

"Let me grab my things—" The blond-haired man with the odd cowlick was already moving. "—cause time is tight to do this. And I want to do it."

Garik had his shoes on, and he followed Devon into the other room. Joseph and Tyrone were gone—the door with them—leaving a gaping wound in one wall. Outside, life was beginning to stir, people heading to the cafeteria via one of the elevators, or others carrying training equipment, readying for a morning of honing their skills in the hope of not being designated as "Level 5" material. The whine of a floor polisher bled in, and for some reason it caught Garik's attention. He'd not considered that, that regular cleaning crews had to do regular cleaning on a regular basis.

Life goes on for some people, even when his didn't. The realization fed his frustration. His earlier remorse evaporated, and he burst out, "Stop it, stop it, stop it!"

Devon had been loading a leather gym bag, and he dropped a pair of socks inside and stood. He cocked his head and fought a smile. "Okay, go on, kiddo."

"It's just that—" Garik felt himself getting louder, and outside the door, he could see the floor polisher. It was finally silent, and the man running it was winding the power cord. He looked Garik's direction, and they locked eyes before the man glanced away and turned his back. Garik fought to control the volume of his emotions as they began to erupt from him into more than he had meant to say. "Nobody tells me anything. I'm right here. A person, not an experiment. You can't just lock me away and expect me to follow along on your leash like a good puppy. If you don't want me, give me to someone who does. Airman Han, what happened to him? He's the only one in this whole place who's even nice to me, and you people stick me with Shan Vang. The man hates me. I'm done with you people."

"Hey, hey, I'm not you people. I can't do anything about the leash, but I don't expect you to be a good puppy. A big bad wolf is more like it. Huff, puff, blow the house down?"

Garik smiled despite his irritation.

"Better, kiddo. You're right. Here's the deal. I've got an extra room in my place in Corona City—well, my office, but it's got a door. Shoate says we can bunk there since your door is toast. I want to get moved. She might change her mind." He winked. "I appreciate your couch, but face it. It's not my dream digs. And I'll try to keep you part of the conversation. Deal?"

"Okay. Do I get a bed?" An office ... it didn't sound like it.

"If you're a good puppy."

Garik frowned and saw Devon break into a smile.

"Gotcha! Already done. Shoate's having a bed delivered sometime today. You get to set it up, though."

"Can I take my ZBoard?" It was the only thing he owned, even if it really belonged to the Tower.

Devon looked at the unit, as if seeing it for the first time. He nodded. "You ride it, and I'll call Joseph to get the charger delivered. But we've got to move. Now."

Finally! Garik slipped it from the charging station, turned it on, and dropped it to the floor. Devon already had his bag over his shoulder, and Garik followed him out the door.

To discover what, he wasn't entirely sure.

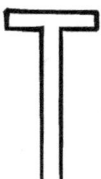

— 2 —

he schedule for the morning fell apart two turns in.

Passing the emergency clinic and swinging by the recreation area for Devon to access the latest updates on his morning assignments, they were accosted by two human hybrids making their way to the clinic. The first was Stephen Klandermans, a man with wide shoulders, kinky blond hair in wiry dreads, and amused gray eyes. His clothes were a tumble of well-worn fabrics with frayed edges. He was helping Ineke Van Stekelenburg, a tall, slender woman with dark hair and small eyes, who held one arm cradled in the other. She wore an aloof expression creased with pain.

Stephen flashed a bright smile, easy and natural, and he called, "Hey, Dev. See you've got the little jail-breaker along for a ride."

"Party-hardy, Stephen," Devon returned. "What's with Ineke?"

Jail-breaker? Garik swelled up. And what was with the woman? She looked as though she could burn a hole in his brain. Perhaps she could. He'd seen weirder things in Corona Tower's basement research complex.

"The thing wrong with Ineke is Stephen." Ineke overenunciated, as though making a point with her speaking style. As though no one else would understand if she didn't explain it in the simplest terms.

"Me, yah!" Stephen laughed and waved one hand in the air. "I did a somersault, showing off, and, um, well, I didn't know—"

"He hit my arm and we must visit the clinic for a splint. I will likely not attend my session tomorrow, Devon. I apologize in advance." Ineke nodded to him.

"Not my fault, not really. You were in my way, Ineke. Promise, Dev." His face said he found this amusing, and he turned to Garik. "And I want to hear all about your time outside, little guy. Last night, the big man had good things to say about you. And I like the skaterboard." He nodded to Garik with a grin before making soothing sounds to Ineke and continuing past them towards the emergency clinic.

"Jail-breaker?" That and skaterboard. Garik stepped from the ZBoard, lifted the end and balanced it at his side. The word reminded him of Arik, rancid in his memory.

"Come on, kiddo. I don't know what was said in the meeting, 'cause us ordinary people aren't allowed, but do you really think no one tracked you and your cadre of late-night escapees all day yesterday? Me, I'm not allowed an opinion. I'm not one of you, but for everyone else, you were the entertainment of the day."

"Sheesh." Garik had to stop himself from lashing out in frustration. If he had been the entertainment of the day, that changed his relationship to everyone he saw in the corridors. He might not know them, but they likely knew him and everything that had happened to him—and was likely the reason Rodheimer hadn't felt it necessary to explain who Garik was last night when he praised him. He also expected they all had an opinion of him they would love to share. Great! He was looking forward to that!

"Okay, since we're good on that, let me pull my updates to see what hasn't been uploaded to the Tower's net." Devon pulled several sheets of paper from a message box and laid them on a counter. He began entering the changes into his watch.

Garik observed him without really seeing what he was doing, instead picturing John Carter's black-faced watch the night they were escaping. *The night they were escaping*—it was only the night before last. It seemed days and weeks, and Garik immensely missed those he had bonded with during his bid for freedom. His concern for them battled with his dismay that he was back in the basement complex and had a jailer assigned to him full time, and he forced himself to shake off the feeling. It didn't benefit him now, and he refocused on how anyone down here could know about his time outside. John Carter's watch had only accessed the real Internet once they were outside the basement complex. The Tower wouldn't post updates, not on the Tower's internal net, at least not until they were sure he had been recaptured, and even then, what about the twelve people still on the outside? That wasn't something the Tower would want widely known. It would come across as a failure, and who wants people tagging and following their failures?

So, how was it possible that people had followed his escape, and more depressingly, his recapture?

Devon had returned the papers and picked up his bag. Two people with similar facial structures came running toward them.

"Jacquelien, Bert." Devon greeted them, as if he expected them to continue by.

Instead, they stopped, glanced at Garik and nodded as if they knew him, and the woman placed a hand on Devon's arm. She boasted a red line tattooed from her widow's peak down her nose, past her lips, along her chin and neck, and disappearing into her shirt. When she opened her mouth to speak, the red line broke for the first time.

"Devon, it's—"

"—Ineke." The man finished her sentence. He wore his hair shaved over his right ear, and it tumbled into a bristly waterfall on the left. Black tatts across his upper torso moved underneath a long-sleeved black shirt made mostly of netting. His chocolate jaw sported a darker shadow of bristly black.

"I just spoke with her and Stephen."

"And we all know—"

"—Stephen."

Garik looked from one to the other and tried to figure out the pair. They talked over one another, finishing one another's sentences, as though it were natural to them. They couldn't be twins. She was blonde as Devon, and he was breakfast cocoa. Yet, they looked similar. Same DNA source? What other possibility was there? Did the looniness in this place never end?

"And we want you—"

"—to come with us."

"An injury report. You can—"

"—shortcut the red tape."

"If you have—"

"—the time, of course."

Garik's head spun. Did they have their brains linked? Was this a DNA-hybrid experiment in telepathy or something? A voice from around the corner called, "Bert? Ineke with you?"

Bert called, "Nah, Veronika! At the clinic. But the amazing escape artist is here! Let everyone know!" He grinned at Garik.

"As for going with you, I'm baby—" Devon cut off his word and glanced at Garik. "I have Garik with me today. I can't leave him. Sorry."

Babysitting! How could Devon say that? It might be true, but it sounded so childish! Jailer was more accurate, though he supposed it would be equally irritating. And, who was Veronika? She remained a voice only.

"Bring him—" Bert winked.

"—with you. Lansana is—" Jacquelien added.

"—meeting us there." Bert nodded in collusion.

Devon glanced at his watch, tapped it, and took a deep breath, thinking, and released it. "I've got Paul on my schedule. I can come, but I won't have long."

"As long as you need." A new voice, deeper, and a man—a woman?—appeared out of the wall next to Jacquelien and Bert, almost as if his/her skin had taken on the texture and color of the background surface and then had decided to look human once more. Large lips and dusky skin seemed eminently feminine, but the voice said otherwise. After a moment, beaded clothes in bright South African colors and patterns flickered into substance around him.

"How did you, um," Garik shivered, "do that?"

"You must be Garik." The man laughed, revealing gold letters inset into his front two teeth. "Paul Gberie. You didn't see me last night at the meeting. Obviously." He winked at his joke. "How did you escape from the Tower's dungeon?"

"Um, but you, you weren't here a few moments ago!"

"Of course I was here. You should be asking why you couldn't see me. And Devon, consider this my session with you. I also want to know Ineke's tale. Or is it tail?"

Paul began to laugh uproariously, and the other three rolled their eyes and shook their heads.

Garik had missed something. The man, invisible or not . . . he should have been able to hear him approach. Even invisible people made noise when they moved. He wondered how long before Paul disappeared again. And if he would be able to track him by listening when he did.

STEPHEN WAS taping Ineke's arm into a splint when Garik and Devon entered the emergency clinic. Stephen was cracking a joke about Humpty Dumpty, and Ineke tried to silence him with a bored expression and her eyes on a light fixture on the ceiling.

"Not working, Ineke?" Devon chuckled.

"Don't start," she growled, her face pale with pain.

As Stephen finished up the job, an infusion of new

people was a tidal wave sweeping Garik along with each introduction, whether formal or contextual.

Lansana was Lansana Opoku-Mensa, wearing patterned scarification on her face in a double line circling each eye and running up her forehead. Her head was shaved and balanced on a neck too long to seem real. She stepped in, nodded to each person present—including Garik—but didn't speak. She seemed to be evaluating the situation, a smart move, in Garik's eyes.

Jacquelien and Bert were Jacquelien Van Kessel and Bert Ellis. They were so interwoven that even their actions seemed coordinated. One would move, and the other completed the motion, just as when they had been talking earlier in the corridor.

Veronika Abbink entranced Garik. Not like love, but like a beautiful sunset that was too astounding to comprehend. Oversized earrings draped from her ears, and her teeth commanded her face when she smiled, but that wasn't what fascinated him. Nor were her messenger bag and the bright, neon colors she covered herself with. Her skin seemed to reflect the hue of whatever she was near, at one point changing before Garik's eyes so subtly he might not have noticed if he wasn't looking.

Benjamin Fuest was quite ordinary, and Garik doubted he was modified. A scraggly beard enclosing a small mouth, large forehead, and heavy eyebrows . . . but his face lit up when he smiled, changing him completely.

The final person to join them introduced himself to Garik with a precise offering of his hand. Zekeria Salem. He looked fourteen, with bowl-cut hair and brown eyes. At first glance, Garik thought he saw through what looked like posturing. Then Zekeria turned his head to reveal a crisp profile, and he smiled to bring the picture to photographic perfection. Immediately, Garik understood. Zekeria knew how to present himself for the best impression. A learned skill or DNA-based, he had no idea, but it worked. Zekeria sealed the connection by saying, "I am Zekeria. I'm sorry that we all know you and you know none of us. Please be patient. We're not as weird as we seem."

You may not be, Garik thought. The rest? He had them pinned perfectly. Weird was the word. He hadn't felt inclined to give them any leeway, but Zekeria's words worked their magic on him, and he smiled back.

"Thank you. There's one thing I'd like to know. How was everyone able to follow my escape—"

Garik didn't get to finish his question. Ineke slumped in her chair, and before Stephen could stop her, she slipped through his hands and tumbled to the floor, hitting her head and spraying blood across the tile.

"I said this was a bad idea. Hospital, I said. No one listens to me." Benjamin twisted his hands and looked out the door.

Paul shrugged, and as if by magic, took on the texture and color of the wall behind him. A moment later, his beaded outfit seemed to twinkle, and it shimmered into nothingness.

"Oh, Ineke. Everyone, we need to coordinate, get Ineke to the hospital. Can someone get a gurney to carry her?" Veronika knelt by Ineke, and soon others joined her, and the injured woman vanished from view. "Girlfriend, we've got you covered. We're with you."

Zekeria puffed out his cheeks. "Let me think. Ineke down. This might not look good for Stephen. Bert and Jacquelien, you have your passkeys back?"

Back. Garik understood. They had been punished for something. Still, the woman was just lying there. He could carry her. Before he could offer, the situation changed.

"Ah, my little South African team." Weston Rodheimer, surprisingly quiet for such a large man, startled Garik. "There you are, Devon. How is your new companion behaving? I hear you are transferring quarters."

Garik swallowed hard. Transferring to Devon's place, and in a rush so no one would stop them. Was Rodheimer angry or pleased? Was it his time to face the electrified sword?

His tried to steady his nerves, but they were running down his back in cold rivulets of tingling sweat, and it was too late to recall them.

— 3 —

evon palmed his door. When it unlocked, he removed his passkey and stepped through.

Watching, Garik recalled Marisa using Halo Sunchaser's passkey the night before Garik was forced into the human-hybrid project. They had learned that a fresh palm scanner update was required every three hours. Garik's passkey—*the one he used to have*—hadn't required him to use the palm scanners. It also hadn't allowed him access to the elevators that would take him up into the daylight of the real world, so that explained that.

During their interaction with the Director, he had been certain that the big man would confiscate all their passkeys, but Rodheimer, surprisingly, had been less brutal than expected. Near to friendly, at least toward Garik, asking about the reasons they were moving to Devon's quarters and offering to speak to Joseph Howard to see if the repairs to Garik's door could be optimized in any way. Devon had mentioned Lt. Shoate's connection, and the Director had paused and asked, "Lt. June Shoate?" At Devon's nod, he said, "I will make a point to offer my appreciation for her initiative in handling this," before he ran his eyes over each person crowded into the emergency clinic and vanished.

Garik was certain each of the people with him had felt the big man looking into their souls to see if they qualified for continued existence in the human-hybrid project, or if he should sic Halo Sunchaser on them now and end their paltry lives before they sank any lower into banal and useless debasement.

Devon dropped his bag onto a nubby textured couch, and he dropped beside it, his legs splayed and his head back. "Whew, thought I was gonna be toast there."

"You should have been at the party last night." Garik's back still crawled with wet, and his heart hadn't settled yet. "My room?"

"There." Devon pointed to the back of the kitchen. A door revealed a darkened cavern. "There's no bed, yet, and I'll need to make space for you, but it's yours. Check it out if you want."

Garik wanted. After Bert and Jacquelien had returned with a gurney and Ineke was trundled off to the elevator to head two floors down to the hospital, Devon had excused the two of them, and they had worked their way through the various corridors leading to Corona City. Windows mocked the illusion of inside and out, a pretense that was as near to aboveground as the underground facility offered, with two parks, a pool that looked like it was outside, and wide streets planted with shrubs and flowers. The closer they got, the more ordinary the people looked, office workers, scientists who had come from abroad to work in the research program, and people like Devon who weren't hybridized but were necessary to work with those who were. Garik stood his ZBoard just inside the door to the apartment and stepped past the small kitchen.

"You live here all the time?"

"Free lodgings, so sure. Why?"

"No reason, just that not everyone does, right?" The underground parking garage. It was huge. Someone had to be parking in all those spaces. There were the people who lived in the Tower, but they had the parking garage above ground.

"Not everyone." Devon's eyes were still closed.

"Okay. You can leave when you want, though, right?"

"If I want."

"Okay," Garik repeated. He hit the switch and light filled the room. A chair, a small desk, and a computer. A bookshelf with a few pictures, one of a pretty blonde woman in ski gear, and Garik remembered Devon telling him about his mother. Another photo of her revealed a ski slope in the background with an Olympic logo to the side. "Your mother was pretty."

"Thanks. I'll put all that away for you. You can set out what you want." Devon had come up behind him and tapped him on the shoulder to let him around.

"Sure." Garik moved aside as Devon stepped inside, and the blond man opened a box and took out a medal. He held it out for Garik to take.

"Silver for ski jumping. I was just a kid, but I remember how proud she was of that."

"You can leave it out. Everything, actually. I don't have anything to bring with me." Garik stroked the raised image with his fingers before handing it back. "How long till your next session? I'm hungry."

"I said you should have eaten, kiddo." Devon grasped the back of Garik's neck, ran his hand up to tousle his hair, and grinned. "But yeah, raid the fridge. There's likely something in there."

Devon disappeared, and soon, Garik could hear a shower running. He turned back to the kitchen and the living room. Devon had carried his bag into wherever he was, although with the running water, that was obvious. A door across the entry revealed a bed—Devon's room—and a closed door leaking the sound of the water. Was there a second bathroom? Unlikely. He could wait.

Passing the entry door, he tried the handle to see if it would open. Locked. He should have known. At the window, he lifted a blind. At least it was real. Outside, a woman in a nurse's smock walked confidently by, and after a moment, two men, one laughing at something the other one said.

Garik dropped onto the couch, at the opposite end from where Devon had been, and he looked around. A television and a gaming unit. He leaned his head back and closed his eyes.

What was happening *out there*? That's what he wanted to know. What about his friends, Jantzen and Paolo and Joanie and all the rest? How was Marisa? She had said she missed him, too. She wouldn't have betrayed him without a good reason. No way. And Leigh, Laura, and John. Justin, with his new wings, out and flying over the city. Garik would like wings about now, to fly away from this place. He would wait until an event on the mall, then rip off his shirt and fly away, all the way away till no one knew where he was.

He couldn't, and his eyes burned. He was part wolf, and what could a wolf do? He wasn't even turning into anything special. Jantzen, purple mist. Paolo, steaming jets of water from his fingertips. Joanie, well, no one could prove she could come back to life, but still, better than nothing.

Thanks, Director. I'm a dud and it's all your fault.

Something dinged, and Garik felt between the cushions. He pulled out a MicroArt tablet. It had a message on the screen.

"Hey, Dev. My dad's in for an emergency treatment. I need a ride to the hospital at lunch. See you out front. Have you logged into your social media? Check out this link."

Garik immediately knew. This device had full access to the outside world. He looked toward Devon's room and could still hear the shower. He had to do this now. He stood, moved toward his new room, and inside, he closed the door. He clicked and enlarged the image playing on the screen and his heart began to pound.

There he was, running along Avenue C, with the Cowden Street overpass just in front of him. The light changed, and he was off. The image jittered and changed perspective, likely drone footage, then zeroed in on Garik just as a uniformed man fired a BolaWrap his direction, and down Garik went, hard on the pavement. His newly acquired sunglasses skittered sideways, and his head hit the pavement once, then twice, and he lay still.

Garik felt jittery, his movements jerky, a puppet of his nerves as he returned to the couch and replaced the device where he found it. He had to get control so Devon didn't suspect what he knew. Of course, there was a link to the outside. Just that not everyone could access it, meaning not Garik, except . . . he had, even if he wasn't supposed to. It made sense now that he thought about it. Devon wasn't part of the program, not one of the hybridized humans being experimented on to force them to be something no human was designed to be. Devon could come and go when he wanted. Of course, he could link to information beyond the concrete and steel walls that kept the hybrids safely imprisoned in their subterranean depths.

Who else, he wondered? If only he could contact Airman Han. They had a connection, his Street Strider. He was certain the man would help him if he could.

Devon appeared, his blond hair wet and glistening, his cowlick as energetic as ever, and a towel wrapped around his waist.

"Did you eat, kiddo?" He pulled a juice box from the fridge, poked it with a straw and sucked on it.

"About to." The Internet, he wanted to say. What's happening out there? His heart pounded at the thought he might lose the meager access he'd just viewed. He hoped Devon didn't remember the device, say, "Oh, I forgot to put this away," and lock him out.

Garik moved in front of the couch and willed Devon not to look.

"A banana. I eat healthy, so I always have fruit.

Have one." Devon broke one off and held it out.

"Thanks." Garik took it and began to peel it, all the time hiding the device in the couch, pleading with Devon to not remember it was there. The fruit was a hard lump in his throat, and it felt it wanted to come back up.

"You feeling okay?" He tossed his empty box in the trash.

"I'm fine." Garik forced a smile and dropped onto the couch. The MicroArt tablet cut into his back, and he forced himself to relax. "Just wanting to get out there and see what we're doing today. I'm excited to see what you teach some of the other participants."

"That's the attitude." Devon winked and made a quick fist and released it. "I knew you'd come around. Okay, kiddo, you wait right there, and I'll toss on some clothes. Got so much planned today, your eyes'll be spinning by the time we get back."

"Leave me energy enough to put my bed together!" Garik scrunched one side of his face into a return wink and held out a hand with his thumb raised. "Don't want to sleep on your couch tonight."

"Right-o, kiddo. I got'cha there." Devon grinned and disappeared into the bedroom, this time closing off the room from view.

Garik reached behind him and pulled out the tablet. He didn't power on the screen, just looked at it longingly and stroked it along one edge. *Marisa,* he thought.

Everyone else he knew, too, but Marisa was most on his mind. He heard the door across the room, and he slipped the tablet under the couch and stood.

"Riding the board?" Devon was gathering his things and slipping them in various pockets. His fanny pack was bulging and off to the side. He nodded at the ZBoard.

"Sure." Garik shrugged. The board connected him to who he used to be, even if he would have laughed at it before his induction into the Tower's basement world.

"Will it need a charge? Joseph and Tyrone can't get the charger here before the afternoon." The fanny pack was going on, and Devon glanced around the room as he adjusted it.

"Not unless we're going more than twenty miles. Are we?"

"No. Downstairs to the training cells." Devon unzipped his fanny pack and began looking through it.

"Leave someone's shoes out?" Garik threw it out like a joke, remembering the first time they'd met, and Devon had pulled out a pair of climbing shoes for him to use.

"I have a tablet. I was using it before I was sent to your place . . . anyway, it's gone missing. It has an app for messaging that I use. Have you seen it?"

"Let me look." Garik turned in a full circle, making a show of taking in every surface, and shrugged. "What does it look like?"

"The size of my hand." He spread his fingers wide to approximate the MicroArt tablet now under the couch. "Not to worry. I can survive without it. I have my watch, after all." Devon held up one arm, stretched his hand until his watch appeared out of his sleeve, and grinned.

"Then I'm not worrying. Here, I've got the door. You look like your hands are full." Garik could hardly keep his eyes from the couch. He wanted to look so badly, just to reassure himself the tablet couldn't be seen.

"Not too full for this." Devon worked out his pass-key from a small pocket and held it out. "Insert that for me, and I'll take care of the scanner."

Garik slipped it in the panel and stepped aside. Devon pressed his hand to the sensor, and an internal light traveled from top to bottom and back again. The door unlocked, thump, thump, a sound Garik had grown familiar with, and he removed the key and offered it back to Devon, who nodded in thanks and made it disappear.

Three hours. Three hours before Devon's key would require his palm to be scanned again. Garik wondered if that applied to any door the key worked. When Marisa had used Halo Sunchaser's stolen key, it had given them three hours of freedom to explore every door they wished, including the one in the main elevator that led from Corona Tower directly into the forbidden basements. If the passkeys would lead them down, it likely would allow them back up again.

As they exited the apartment onto the brightly normal street that was really a spacious corridor, Garik's attention was focused a hundred percent on Devon's pocket, hoping, just hoping that the key would fall out, he could scoop it up, and he could Houdini this place once more. Then the wheel of his ZBoard caught a small curb encircling a border of planted and well-tended zinnias, and Garik nearly went down. Devon glanced at him, but he was preoccupied with checking his watch, and when he saw Garik had recovered, he nodded his approval and returned to his watch.

Outside, outside, outside. Garik could hardly think of anything else, even to pay attention to where he was riding. He separated his thoughts into now and wish. Devon's passkey would be best, even as he accepted the unlikely possibility of it falling from the man's pocket. The tablet, however, that was real. He had watched drone footage of his capture. He was out there, on the net, and that meant someone knew he was here, or at least that he had been in the city, and now he was vanished. Not had vanished, but was vanished, as in wiped from the city clean as a whistle.

It's all lies, he wanted to shout. I didn't go anywhere. I should be in class at Bay City High with my friends, getting fries on the mall, visiting with Marisa under the stars on the roof of our apartment building. Weston Rodheimer and his goons had stolen that from him, and he'd received nothing in return.

Except a shaved head, now thankfully regrown. And he'd met some new friends, but that didn't change things.

He sent a silent message to everyone in the city, "I'm here! Under your feet! Look hard enough, and you'll find me!"

Then Devon inserted his passkey into the main elevator, the door dinged, and it opened wide.

"You, first." Devon smiled as if Garik had a choice.

"Thank you." Garik stepped inside. *Play by the book, part of the pack. It's the only way to escape the game.*

The door dinged and closed, crushing Garik's hopes, and the car began to move downward.

Garik gave himself up to what he couldn't control, and despair drained the light from around him.

$$-\,4\,-$$

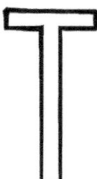

he cryptic text on the MicroArt tablet was forgotten in the onslaught of Devon's first training session.

The door to the training cell began to swing shut as Devon dropped his things—including his fanny pack—on a sturdy metal table and took quick steps across the room to a row of lockers. The door latched with the metallic double thump of steel locking steel, and a green light just above it winked on.

Silence numbed every auditory sensation.

"What's with the—" Garik cut himself off, perplexed. He could barely hear himself speak. He yelled to Devon, "What's with the sound?"

"Active sound absorption. The sessions can get loud." Devon yelled back, and still, he sounded two blocks away. "Wait right there. We can talk in a minute."

Garik became aware of the textured surfaces of the walls. Part of the active sound absorption. Devon returned and set a case on the table. Inside gleamed several weapons, including two knives, two air pistols, and the glinting steel of a finely honed sword.

"Swordplay?" Garik's voice had a dull, closed-in sound, like his words were trapped and unable to escape more than a few inches from his face.

"Of a sort." Devon's voice was equally flat, caged to the space just around his head.

The door vibrated, thunk, thunk, and opened. The ambient sounds around them brightened, became real again. The green light above the door turned red. Garik got it. With the door open, the active sound absorption stopped. Closed, it was on. Lansana Opoku-Mensah with her shaved head and scarification around her eyes stepped through. She swiveled her head left, then right, evaluating the room, even though she had likely been here multiple times.

She tilted her head on her long neck. "Garik. Are we ready to start, Devon?"

Devon didn't answer. Instead, he lifted one of the knives, flipped it in his hand to grasp the blade, and flung it hard at Lansana. She ducked just before the blade of the knife buried itself in the wall.

"What—" Garik sputtered, but before he could say more, Lansana interrupted him with a grin.

"Faster. I'm better than that."

"Dodge this, kiddo!" Devon had the other knife and flipped it across the room. Lansana had already started to move before the knife left his hand, and he aimed where she was heading, not where she was. The knife lunged for her as if seeking her flesh with a mind of its own.

Garik instinctively moved—to do what, he didn't know—and rainbows began to shimmer around each item in the room. Lansana and the knife slowed to a crawl, and Devon held aloft a frozen hand to stop Garik from interfering. Garik leaped across the training cell, covering nearly twelve feet in a single burst. Twisting his body, he hit the hilt of the knife with his elbow, sending it skewing to the side and spinning through the air.

Garik landed in a heap on the far side of the room. The rainbows disappeared, the knife clattered to a stop on the floor, Lansana looked from Garik to the knife, and Devon still held out his hand to prevent Garik from interfering.

"Whoa!" Devon's eyes went wide. "What was that, kiddo?"

"I'm cold." Garik burned with the ice surrounding

him. The muted sound in the room made him feel even colder. He was surprised to see his skin wasn't frosted with crystals. "I think I should have eaten more than a banana for breakfast."

"Timber wolf. Very fast. My turn. Devon? The guns, next?" Lansana had evaluated the situation, determined that everyone was okay, and was ready to resume her session.

"Why are you trying to kill her?" Garik tried to stand, and he made it to his knees, breathing hard.

"Can't." Devon lifted one of the guns and, before Garik could react, released a pellet that caught Lansana directly in the shoulder. She twisted, hitting the wall with the impacted shoulder, only to straighten and say, "Again."

"How—" No blood! How could that be?

"Lansana's armored." Devon grinned like a schoolboy, the cowlick at his temple adding to the image. "Pangolin DNA. Armored anteater. Watch."

Lansana leaped, and Devon chased her with his pellets, impacting about a quarter of the time. She seemed to brush off each impact as if it were an insect bite.

Garik's eyes followed the interplay, and when they were finished showing off, he called, "The knife. You can't tell me that wouldn't have done damage."

Lansana looked hard at Devon, and the man dove for the knife on the floor and flung it her direction. She didn't try to dodge this time. She hit the incoming blade with her fist, sending it clattering Garik's direction. When it stopped spinning on the floor, he looked at it to see the blade crumpled along the cutting edge.

Then Devon's watch chimed, a tiny *chink* with the active sound dampening, and he said, "Excuse me while I take this." He slipped an earbud into one ear and tapped the watch before turning away to take the call.

Lansana offered Garik a hand to stand. It was the one she had used to bat away the knife. There was no damage to her skin at all.

Garik smiled in thanks and let her pull him to his feet. At least he could finally stand, even if he didn't understand everything. He guessed it was time to accept that likely he never would.

MOMENTS LATER, Devon grabbed his fanny pack, made a beeline to the door, inserted his passkey, and released the seal. The light above the door turned red, and real sound returned.

"Apologies, Lansana. I've got to be somewhere. We can reschedule. Garik, kiddo, tuck in and follow me."

Garik found he could barely wobble. He wasn't sure about the rainbow thing, but each time it happened, it walloped his stamina. He waved to Lansana and focused on keeping up. Devon seemed in an unaccountable rush.

"I knew I should have searched harder for my tablet," the rec director called from down the corridor.

Garik dropped his skateboard to the floor and pictured the tablet on the floor under the couch. He remembered the message. *I need a ride to the hospital at lunch.* Maybe he should have revealed it, but he needed it to access the Internet. The tablet had shown him the unexpected bonus of the video footage. Outside! How could he give up that possibility?

"So, where are we going?" Garik had caught up, thanks to the ZBoard, and he slowed to match Devon's rapid pace.

"An acquaintance from the Tower. Do you know Gunther Diehl?"

"Sure, the concierge. We've met."

"I thought so. He matched me up with a resident—"

"From Stamford Suites, right?"

"Right-o, kiddo." Devon looked surprised. "This resident needs coverage sometimes, and being from out of town . . ." Devon shrugged, and he inserted his passkey in the elevator access panel. "The extra cash money doesn't hurt."

"Yeah. I've done that." Garik had grown up poor—and still was, as he had no money at all, now—and he understood taking on extra jobs when they were available. "What do you have to do for him?"

The elevator doors closed, and Devon seemed to see Garik for the first time since leaving the training cell. He hit his forehead with the heel of his hand. "Oh, man, how did I not think of this?"

"What?"

"You." Devon let out a hard breath.

It clicked for Garik. *Ride to the hospital. See you out front.* This was perfect.

"I can stay in your apartment. I won't mess with any of your things, and I can't get in any trouble." The tablet. Locked in, he would have all the time he wanted to explore.

"I thought of that. No time." Devon checked his watch and pulled out a key fob. "Already late, so you're with me. Be good. I'm not supposed to have you off campus." The elevator dinged and the doors opened to the main lobby. He sighed. "Why do they do this to me? Act natural and stay close to my side so there are no questions. Got it?" Devon gave him a firm look.

"Got it."

"Okay, kiddo, let's go." Devon moved forward, and he called and waved to several people. They passed the main cafeteria, the one Garik normally visited at mealtimes, and headed down an unfamiliar corridor—to Garik, at least. Devon paused at a door with a wire-reinforced glass window, inserted his passkey, and the door prompted him for his hand. He looked at Garik. "They don't let just anyone outside. Sorry, kiddo. Stick close." He pressed his hand, the door unlatched, thump, thump, and Garik kicked his ZBoard up to grab the end. He followed Devon into the bowels of the very familiar underground parking garage where he and his friends had been only two nights earlier as they had made their escape from Corona Tower.

Overhead lights flooded the space. Vast rows of cars stretched into the distance, tightly packed closer to the elevator. Farther away, they thinned, but Garik estimated hundreds, at least. Worker bees, working for the money, serving the Tower to do what needed to be done. He hated to group Devon with those people, but then . . . and he let go of that thought. Devon wasn't bad, not like some people he'd met in the Tower's dungeon.

Devon's car was an older Merc hatch, with the tri-star proudly displayed in the fake grille. Devon beeped it to unlock it, unplugged the power cord, stashed it in the hatch with Garik's board, and leaned the seat forward for Garik to climb into the back. The rear windows were deeply tinted. He shrugged. "Sorry."

As the car moved away, emanating the faint whine of electric motors, the light from the ramp leading to the outside world grew closer. This time, the gates opened for Devon pretty as you please, unlike Garik's previous journey up the ramp two days before. They entered the street, turning right on Stamford, the same direction Garik had driven in Kevin Lee's van. A normal world, two days gone, and a million lightyears away.

"Where are we headed?"

"The high school. Then Bay City Medical." Devon

drummed the steering wheel as he waited at the light to go left on Corona. "Sorry if I'm jittery. This is way outside my pay grade. If that tablet hadn't gotten lost . . . but I can't fix that, so here we are. Just keep your head low. You being out here is my job if you're seen." The light changed, and Devon made his left, heading towards Park Avenue.

"So, I can't just jump out and you say you don't know where I went?" Garik teased, even though it was exactly what he'd been thinking. He suspected that was why he was in the back seat.

Devon slammed the brakes. Another car honked, and Devon ignored it as he turned to glare at Garik. "I've been good to you, kiddo. How can you suggest that? I wouldn't just get fired. I'd be blacklisted from every job Rodheimer had any control over me getting with any company in the world."

"Sorry."

"Okay. I apologize for biting your head off. Like I said, I'm jittery with you out here, so head down, and let's do this. Okay?"

"Sure, kiddo." Garik kicked underneath Devon's seat. When the man looked in the mirror, Garik grinned and gave him a thumb's up.

"I'm never having kids, ever," Devon muttered.

I can hear you, Garik thought. Still, in the cause of not getting his head bitten off again, he didn't say it. Even a seventeen-year-old knows how to use wisdom occasionally.

GARIK'S BIG surprise came when Devon pulled up in front of the school and his passenger climbed in the car. The high schooler fell inside, pulled off a knit cap, and said, "Thank you. I texted you this morning, but you surely missed it. I am happy I found your number stored in my watch." He lifted a hand to his thick shock of tousled hair to sort it out, then brushed his palms along the sides where it was cut short.

"Dieter?" Garik leaned forward and smashed the familiar youth on his shoulder with a fist.

"Ah, my friend." Dieter's face lit up when he saw Garik. "You were disappeared when I returned from school. You, my friend, are blowing up the social media. Boom!" He put his palms together and exploded them apart.

"You two know each other?" Devon seemed to melt, and his face turned paler than arctic ice.

"We are the best of friends!" Dieter held up a fist for Garik to bump. "No one can argue otherwise. Is that not so?"

Garik bumped the fist. What else could he do but agree?

— 5 —

evon took Fourth south from the high school, bypassing Central Park and coming up alongside The Martial Arts Center. The two teens talked skateboards while Devon drove white-lipped and refused to look to either side. Instead of taking Ninth east along the front of the Center, when the light changed, he accelerated toward the next intersection at Lilac.

"Should you not turn here? Ninth is less slow. My father does not enjoy traffic lights." The street sign for Ninth faded behind them.

"Less slow but obvious," Devon muttered, as he

reached Lilac, turned left, and accelerated.

Garik would have preferred taking Ninth along the front of the Center, although Devon was correct. The Center's parking lot was filled with people squeezing in a practice session on their lunch hour. Lilac would require stops at each street along the way, but the streets would likely be clear of pedestrians.

"Sure. I am not the one driving." Dieter shrugged and gave Garik his attention. "This, let me show you this small movie, a drone shot, I think it is called." He pulled off his watch and held it out to Garik with a grin.

"A drone shot," Garik repeated, and he took the watch. He imagined the video clip from that morning, and a razor shard of guilt twisted in his gut for not telling Devon he had hidden his tablet.

"I did send it to Devon, but since he did not receive the text, I am confident you did not view it. The play arrow, smash it to enjoy your movie."

"Thanks." Garik fell back into the seat and tapped the watch's face, uncomfortable for not being transparent, and the video from that morning began to play. He studied it intently, hoping to see something new. After it finished, he offered the watch back to Dieter, too overwhelmed by the memory of the events to speak.

"So many views." Excitement sparkled in Dieter's eyes. "Did you see? Many thousands. I did not know I was a friend to someone so popular. All over school, everyone sending your video to everyone else. In one class, the teacher stopped teaching and asked what we were doing. He said it was a current event and allowed it to play on the wall screen. You are a hit, my friend. What do you think of that?"

"On the wall screen, like a projector?" Devon was pulling up to make a right on Industrial, which would lead them directly to the Medical Center, and he blew out his cheeks in a huge sigh. He glanced in the rearview mirror and studied Garik. "What else? Your picture on a billboard? There's no way I'm getting you back to the Tower without being seen."

"You are going back?" Dieter leaned over the seat and smashed Garik's knee with a fist. "You are here. Stay. Muhammad and Ibn will be filled with happiness that you have not disappeared once again. I am excited to tell them."

"No, Dieter, you absolutely cannot. I'm in big trouble if you do." Red streaks painted Devon's neck, and they were crawling into his cheeks. "This can't get any worse."

He drove blindingly fast, covering the next three blocks from Lilac before getting caught at the light at Pansy. He slammed the brakes, skidding the tires. A car pulled up on the right. Devon ducked into his seat, but the car turned and pulled away as though nothing was the matter.

One block ahead, the main entrance to the Bay City Medical complex on the left framed the group of medical buildings and their tall, elaborately landscaped masonry backdrop of a wall. The wall separated the hospital from the industrial park two blocks farther down.

The shifting colors of a large television in a display window to the left caught their eye. They couldn't hear the newscaster, but across the top it said Bay City Noon News. The words scrolling across the bottom of the screen said more.

Bay City police, where are you? Yesterday, a local youth was forcefully abducted by armed assailants and whisked away in an unmarked vehicle as seen in this drone footage taken by a local blogger. The video clip from Dieter's watch filled the screen. Garik's face was clearly visible. During the abduction, a superimposed circle appeared around Garik with his name to the side.

"You are on the TV, my friend." Dieter lifted a fist in the air. "Maybe Hollywood, someday. This would never happen in my country. I am filled with more excitement than I thought possible. You must see your friends to tell them you are okay. Your girlfriend, Marisa, surely she would want to know you have not disappeared from her once more."

"I would like that." Garik looked in the mirror. Devon refused to acknowledge him, and the man's face tightened.

Dieter's watch dinged. He touched it and began to read, and he grinned. "Too bad I must leave school, although my father will not think so. Something exciting is being planned, and I would enjoy being part of it."

"I give. What?" Garik leaned forward to read the watch as the light changed, and Devon surged the little Mercedes forward. The electric motors whined in protest.

"A march to the police station with banners and more." Dieter looked up, his eyes shining with anticipation, and when Devon didn't respond, he shifted his enthusiasm to Garik. "Perhaps you can be there, my friend, to show them you are okay—"

"No, he can't." Devon cut him off. "I'm dropping you off at the hospital as requested, and Garik and I are returning to the Tower, which we never should have left." He stomped the brakes at the entrance to the complex with his blinker on, waiting for an especially slow minivan to pass.

"But, that is unfair." Dieter's eyes reflected his astonishment.

Garik agreed. It was very unfair, but Dieter didn't seem to realize that Garik was in the back seat for a reason. He was a prisoner. If he scrambled from the vehicle, where would he run? Devon's life would be ruined, the Tower now knew its weaknesses, and Garik wasn't sure he hadn't been given an implant just for the purpose of tracking him.

Even Garik's friends in the city would be punished

if the Tower thought it would aid their chances in retrieving him, and they wouldn't care who got hurt. The surveillance cameras in The Flower Shop were evidence of that.

Then Devon's phone dinged.

"Now what? Is the Tower planning a protest, too?" He sighed, pulled into a parking space, and placed an earbud in one ear. "Devon speaking."

Dieter had pulled a small phone from his pocket and was typing away. Every few words, he glanced at his watch. He paused, looked at Devon and Garik, grinned, and returned to typing.

"What?" Garik asked. He leaned over the seat, looked at the words Dieter was inputting, and absorbed the impact.

Everyone. See the abducted boy. Lol. We must find a way to rescue him.

Dieter held the phone up, aimed it at Garik, clicked the camera icon, snapped a photo, and asked, "I shall send it?"

Yes, Dieter, send it! Still, it felt cruel to betray Devon. The man had been good to him. But to return to captivity? How could he allow that? There were no good choices. Freedom was so close, but to take it and risk losing it again—

Dieter took the choice from him. He winked, clicked send on his phone, and slipped it in his pocket. His watch chimed, he held it to let Garik see that the message had gone out, and he grinned.

"Thank you, Devon." Dieter released the door with excitement and pushed it open. "My father will be pleased at your help. I will see you later."

Devon, still in conversation, held up a hand for the teen to wait.

"My father will be expecting me. I must go." Dieter threw himself from the car, closed the door, gave Garik a thumbs-up, and took off running for the building.

Devon rolled down the window and called, "Dieter!" When the youth looked back, waved and laughed, then vanished into the caverns of the hospital's interior, he rolled the window back up.

"Can I at least sit up front?" And run away while I'm at it? Garik stuck one shoulder between the seats and reached for the gearshift, popping it with his fingertips.

"The Director is looking for us." Devon took Garik's wrist and returned his arm to the back seat. "That was Airman Vang. The Director has also seen the drone footage. No lunch for you, kiddo."

"Why? I hardly had breakfast."

"I told Vang we were in the cafeteria for lunch. So was he, so I had to lie and say we were in the hospital cafeteria."

"Well, we are at the hospital."

"Yeah, right-o, kiddo, like that's going to fly." Devon had already pulled forward, and he took a right on Industrial. "Van, you remember him? He has direct hospital access, to he's meeting us in the garage so we can take the hospital-only elevator to Level 4. How sick can you pretend to be?"

"I don't know. Why can't you be the sick one?" But Garik understood the man's plan. He wanted to save his skin—understandably—and it might work, if no one tried to match up all the details.

"Do you notice anything here? I'm driving. How sick can I really be?" Devon had the little hatch screaming down First, and with hardly a pause, he hit his blinker, took a right on Park, and pushed the upper limits he could squeeze out of the small car's electric power plant.

"I know how to drive." Garik fell back in his seat. He had driven his Street Strider and Kevin Lee's van. "You don't trust me," he muttered.

Devon didn't answer. He simply shook his head, barely slowed at Ninth, and aimed the nose of the car for Rock Island and the back entrance to Corona Tower.

Garik hardly had time to begin an internal tirade of accusations against the Tower, Weston Rodheimer, and his unwilling induction into the secretive human-hybrid project changing people into military monsters in the Tower's basements when the screech of tires caused him to look up. Daytime running lights filled the window, Devon's little hatchback became an origami project, and the metal skin of the car crumpled around them.

THE GOOD news was that they did make it to the hospital, and the one on Basement Level 4 in the Corona Tower, although by accident. A happy one as far as Devon's future with the Tower was concerned.

The daytime running lights belonged to a large military vehicle driven by Airman Wu Han. Devon had shaved the light at Rock Island a bit too close, and he had charged through the intersection just as the bigger truck rumbled across. The little Mercedes may have crumpled beyond recognition, but the massive bumper on the Airman's truck-like transport was barely scratched.

Airman Han immediately recognized Devon's car. When he saw Garik inside, he made a call to alert the Bay City Police that there had been an accident, but it was a military training exercise, and there was no infrastructure damage. He apologized for not filing permits ahead of time but that they had slipped through the cracks. He had his team attend to the injured passengers, moved the damaged car to a vacant alley for later retrieval, and delivered Devon and Garik to Corona Tower.

Arriving in the parking garage, Airman Han brought the vehicle to a hard stop. Van Hermoso seemed surprised to find Devon severely injured. Garik's clothes looked as bad, but he was sitting up and asking where they were.

"You've been in a car accident. You're injured, so lie still." Airman Han had been driving, and several other people in similar dress were with him.

"I'm fine." Garik saw he was in the back of the vehicle. Devon beside him didn't look so good. A bandage around his head was a red lollipop, and a leg was a pretzel. His own clothes were painted dark crimson, especially one leg of his pants. The pant leg was sliced open, and his leg was wrapped with bandaging. "Can I take this bandage off?"

"Not a good idea." A woman with dark hair and dark eyes and riding in the back seat cautioned him. "Lt. Trenessa Miyoshi." She smiled. "We barely stopped the bleeding."

"I'm fine." Garik hit the bandage with the flat of his hand. "It doesn't even hurt. What about Devon?"

He didn't get an answer. After Van Hermoso realized the extent of Devon's injuries, he paled and called for a backup emergency team from three floors below.

Garik climbed out of the truck, looked back toward the ramp leading outside, and watched the gates to freedom close. He couldn't deal with both that and Devon, and he let it go. The backup medical team arrived, and everyone fell into the elevator with one thought in mind.

Devon had to be saved . . . if he could.

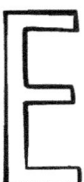

mergency surgery swallowed Devon far into the night. The bigger questions hovering over Garik were how, why, and *what were you doing off-campus with one of the Tower's employees?*

He expected everyone he met to bombard him, to grill him for duplicity, to implode Devon's thinly veiled attempt to cover the broken rules he'd left scattered over the city streets. Instead, he was caged in an examination theater, zapped with high-powered machines, and prodded like a wild animal. *Does this hurt? That? There? How about here?*

During a break in the interrogation, with the room quiet and no one else around, he listened to the forest of voices from through the door. He was certain they were unaware he could hear them, but mostly they weren't saying anything interesting, so he didn't care, until he caught the timbre of Airman Han's voice.

"Yes, we were careful to check for injuries. The young man was unconscious—they both were—and we were unsure of the extent of the injuries—"

"I was certain there was severe damage to the leg." Lt. Trenessa Miyoshi. Garik recognized her voice when she interrupted. She had seemed kind in the transport. "I suppose it could have been the amount of blood. The pant leg was soaked, but clearly, the X-ray proves otherwise." The shrug in her voice was unmistakable.

Garik pressed his fingers into the bronze skin covering his leg. They had cut off the pant leg, leaving him a sort of one-legged pogo boy. He pictured his time in the ring with Justin. The man had opened Garik's arm from the wrist nearly to his elbow, and minutes later, he was completely healed. Jantzen had once said to him, "Don't give away everything you can do." Now he wondered if they were about to discover more than he wanted them to know.

His hearing. He had come to accept that since his infusion with timber wolf DNA, he could hear things no one else could. He was now quicker than he used to be, though he still struggled with understanding the rainbows when he moved too fast. And healing quickly. Devon was in surgery still. How could Garik not have suffered almost as badly?

He suspected he had, only there was nothing now to prove it. Rodheimer might want to convince him that Jantzen was using him for his own purposes, but he trusted one piece of his advice. *Don't give away everything you can do.* He'd already seen the wisdom in that.

The door opened, and Dr. Jimenez stepped through. He smiled and stepped aside as Nurse Ratchett followed him inside and handed him a tablet.

"I'm sure you remember Nurse Fortimer."

"Yes." Not that he wanted to, although she hadn't done anything specific to anger him, more what she hadn't done, like not give him repeated shots of sleepy juice when she didn't want to answer his questions. She was a walking needle in Garik's eyes.

"And who am I?"

"Are you serious?" True, he hadn't seen the man in months, but to ask such a stupid question?

"Just answer the question."

"Dr. Jimenez. How could I forget?"

"Ah." The doctor smiled, perhaps too brightly. "We can confirm your attitude was not damaged in the accident. I wish to talk about the results of your X-rays. First let's discuss bone density and muscle composition . . ."

Garik's mind wandered as the man went on about

calcium absorption, fast twitch muscles, and unusual glucose reserves. His attention perked up when the doctor asked whether recent intense activities had tired him out unusually.

"What sort of intense activities?" In the training cell with Lansana just that morning, he'd dived for the knife, and he'd felt wiped out afterward.

"Sprinting. Jumping. Anything that requires a high level of agility."

Like rescuing the drinks when Rodheimer broke the table, or at the flower shop when evading the Tower goons. Garik processed the memories, and he overlaid them with Jantzen's warning: *Don't give away everything . . .*

"No more than usual." Garik smiled. Say what the man wanted. Anything to be released from this hamster cage. "Can I go now? I think the Director wants to see me."

"I'm sure he does. Your on-line presence is quite the talk about the place."

"Okay, then, I have a question." If the guy was talking, maybe Garik could get something clarified.

"And that is?" Jimenez handed the tablet back to Nurse Fortimer and crossed his arms in front of him, indicating the consultation was nearing its end.

"How come you guys know everything happening out there? Sheesh. I'm always locked out." The doctor frowned, and Garik thought, oops, that didn't come out well.

"That should be obvious. We are not subject to the restrictions of the program participants. As for you, we wish to observe you overnight. Leah will see you to a room." The doctor dismissed Garik and exited.

"Now, my young friend. We need you in the proper clothing for an overnight stay." Leah lifted a sealed pack from a cabinet. "Change into these while I get your room assignment. Leave your old things on the examining table. Don't be slow. I'll be right back." She winked and was gone.

Garik groaned as he pulled his shirt over his head. Inside the package he found a hospital gown and cloth booties with elastic tops. No underwear. No way was he doing that. He would leave them his tattered pants. They were already destroyed. But that was as far down as he was willing to disrobe.

Oh, his socks. They could have them, too. He had no idea what had happened to his shoes.

Changed, he sat on the examining table, and he looked around the neutral and vapid space. Nothing to give it personality or make it memorable. He swung his feet, right, left, bored. Then he heard footsteps outside the door, and he jumped down. When the door opened, he preempted whatever Nurse Ratchett might intend to say.

"What about Devon?"

"What would you like to know?" Nurse Ratchett,

polite but noncommittal.

"Do I get to know how he's doing, or do you people plan to leave me in the dark?" Like, is he still alive?

"His injuries were severe. We're doing what we can. Now, if you'll follow me."

Garik sighed. This was the Nurse Ratchett he recalled. The only thing she hadn't done was give him a shot to put him to sleep. He'd better play nice, or he was certain she would enjoy doing that, too.

LT. TRENESSA Miyoshi appeared the next day to escort Garik to his delayed meeting with Director Weston Rodheimer. On the elevator, he was surprised to see her press the icon for the main lobby of the Tower aboveground.

"I thought I was restricted to the basement." He said it sourly. He had not had a good night, and he still didn't know about Devon.

"Perhaps. That's not my area. We're busy today, and since I helped bring you in yesterday, they assigned me to escort you."

"Too busy for Airman Han?" That's the person Garik wanted to be here. He'd bonded with him over shared Street Strider experiences, and besides, the man had been kind to Garik and his friends, once even offering them breakfast at the food court.

"The Airman is helping in other areas. I'm sorry I can't tell you more. As soon as I drop you off, I'm to join him."

The elevator car dinged, and the doors opened to the vast and sunlit main lobby of the Corona Tower. Miyoshi walked Garik to the Front Desk. Charity Cellers, today in spangly earrings and throwback peach and teal, looked up.

"Mr. Shayk. Lt. Miyoshi. The Director is waiting. You may step through to his office."

"Can I leave the young man with you? I'm assigned to help with the riots—"

Riots? Garik glanced at the display Charity had been watching. People were marching along the waterfront holding placards. *What are they hiding?* Then, *Freedom is a right.* And, *Boycott Chow Down!* There were more, but to boycott Chow Down? Everyone loved Chow Down, the restaurant on the Corona Mall. Outside the expansive wall of windows across the lobby, he could just see the top of the flagpole that normally flew the Bay City High school standard, one of three thrusting skyward for the national, state, and school flags. The wind caught the flag, only it wasn't the one he expected.

A senior prank? It must be. Likely one of his friends, Ibn or Muhammad. The flag popped and shifted in the breeze, but it was without doubt Garik's face from back when his hair was long. Well, longer, as he was working to grow it out again.

His attention returned to the Front Desk as Charity

hung up a phone and said, "Ms. Sunchaser will be right out. You may leave Mr. Shayk with us. Thank you, Lt. Miyoshi."

The lieutenant nodded to Garik, turned, and strode purposefully toward the elevator. The bellhop Choi Bok stepped off, in his standard Corona Towers cream top and tan trousers with a microfiber cloth dangling from his back pocket. He pushed a polished brass cart, now empty, toward the entrance of Stamford Suites, the Tower residence block extending five floors above them. He greeted Gunther Diehl, the concierge, with a respectful nod, before exiting out the double glass doors toward the parking garage.

Halo Sunchaser appeared, saying, "Mr. Shayk, this way. The Director is ready to see you."

Garik's throat was dry. The last time he had seen Sunchaser, she had been wielding her electrified sword, and she had used it to dismember a recalcitrant hybrid mutant one singular atom at a time, until there was nothing at all left.

He tried to calculate, with all serious consideration, just how much longer he had to live.

GARIK EXPECTED Rodheimer to be waiting just off the lobby area. Not so. Sunchaser led him to the elevator, inserted her passkey, and placed her hand on the palm scanner. She chose the penthouse suite, and the door dinged and closed.

"I didn't expect to be invited back to the top." Garik had been there just days earlier. He watched the numbers change, blurring with their speed.

"And you wouldn't be, if not for Mr. Maye's accident." Sunchaser, in her towering headscarf, nearly brushed the mirrored ceiling.

"Yeah, that." Garik heard the rebuke in her words. He had a hard time picturing this elegant, statuesque woman the same as the one two nights ago that had terrorized the hybrids. Yet her tone told the truth of it.

She turned to him, looking down her nose. "Yeah, that," in a mocking lilt. She looked forward once again.

In the penthouse, Rodheimer stood facing outward at the bank of windows wrapping the southeast corner of the building. Sunchaser cleared her throat and said, "The boy, Director."

"Yes, the boy." He didn't turn or otherwise acknowledge Garik's presence.

"Thank you, Director. I'll leave you two." Sunchaser backed away without a word to Garik.

"This way, boy."

Garik moved forward. He noticed that the table Rodheimer had broken last time had been replaced by one in a similar, though not identical style. Unlike the last time Garik was here, the city was washed by the sun, and closer, he could see the roof of Bay City High directly east and the Ransom Building distantly to the south.

"That." Rodheimer didn't have to say what. The flag with Garik's image buffeted in the breeze. "Your doing?"

"Hardly. Remember, you people have me in a strait-jacket."

"A straitjacket." The man glanced at him for the first time. A glint of amusement? It was hard to tell. "Tell me about the training exercise."

"Sure. What training exercise?"

"You, my boy, are wiser than you appear. Never give anything away. I like that about you. Mr. Maye has been an outstanding asset to this facility. I was not aware he was participating in military triage exercises, especially ones that could so easily go awry. One point in his favor. It will be a shame if we lose him."

"Oh, that training exercise." Here it comes.

"And he kept you at his side—and somehow pro-tected you at risk of his own safety. Uninjured as you stand here. Is that how it went?"

Garik's mind raced. Devon. Dieter. Bay City Med-ical Center. Marisa, Ibn, Muhammad, Wu Han . . . until it all ran together, and the Director's tale became the fact that the Director needed it to be.

"Devon always watches over me. He's the best there is." Protect the family, protect the pack, take care of those under his care. Say whatever the man wanted to hear.

"Is that how it went?"

Garik heard the threat in the repeated question. He answered, "Yes, Director Rodheimer. That's exactly how it went."

"That's what I thought. I'll advise Colonel Brace to ease up on Airman Han. Now, we will need to see who else we can arrange to serve as your companion. That, however, can wait for a time, as this has come to my attention. Observe."

Rodheimer lifted a remote and dropped a screen from the ceiling. Light darkening shades around the room hummed as they fell from their hidden recesses, and a projector began to whir. Multiple images appeared on the screen, one of the drone clip Garik had seen earlier, but there were more. The waterfront placards, a large protest march at Central Park, and at each, black-suited enforcement officers with smoked face shields with three glinting metal reinforcement bars running from left to right on the lower half.

"Wow," Garik breathed. "Someone's not happy."

"We—" the Tower, it was clear Rodheimer meant "—like to stay below the radar. Our research facility is off the records. No one, even the city planning department, knows it is there. You are an unknown immigrant who has been successfully deported back to his native Russia. And yet, each of these protests is about you."

"I can't deny the face on the flag, but then I have stupid friends." Thank you, Ibn and Muhammad! I love you! "The rest, what does that have to do with me?"

"That." Rodheimer clicked the remote, and the drone footage grew to eclipse the other three. It looped back to the beginning, and once more, Garik was running at full speed across the bridge to reach the parking lot at Kerre's Dive.

"Not my drone." Garik shrugged.

"Not your drone, not your friends, not about you. I can't prove otherwise, but I do know this." The man's voice darkened as the images on the screen changed, post after post, many with pictures of Tower security, military vehicles going in or out of the parking garage, and others more tightly connected to Garik. He recognized his name in some of them, and others called for an end to the Tower's secrecy. Even Dieter's photograph from yesterday of Garik in Devon's car was there.

"Most of those say nothing about me." Please don't ask about Dieter's picture.

"You think not? If I could, I'd shut down social media across the city. We are the future of this country, and nothing must be allowed to get in the way."

Garik shivered as the burn of the electrified sword crawled across his skin. He hoped it didn't come next for him.

— 7 —

arik's dismissal from Rodheimer's penthouse retreat was a welcome relief.

The man who appeared to accompany him wasn't.

"Mr. Shayk." The elevator doors slipped aside, revealing Senior Airman Shan Vang. He lifted his head slightly and spoke down his nose. "I see we meet again."

"It seems so, Airman." Garik should be accustomed to the man by now, but his stomach clenched. The Airman had repeatedly disparaged him when he thought he couldn't hear. *Useless. Runt. Mongrel.* That last one might have been from a Lt. Wilder. He and Airman Vang had joined Garik and Jantzen in the Tower's elevator to share the ride. They had belittled him in whispers, thinking he couldn't hear. Perhaps a normal human wouldn't have been able to, but then, that wasn't Garik, was it? Now, the words danced through Garik's head anytime Vang was around.

Garik stepped inside and saw a second Airman, a woman with light freckles, reddish-blonde hair, and a tinier waist than Vang's. He nodded at her, wondering what descriptive words they had used about him in the privacy of the elevator.

"Airman," Garik said in greeting, unsure if he should trust her or not.

"Close." She smiled. She glanced at Vang and unmistakably winked before saying to Garik, "Master Sergeant Megan Valladao. One small notch above Airman."

"I suppose I should apologize." Garik was out of apologies. These people should be apologizing to him.

"Your call." She shrugged. "I'd like to observe Airman Vang's interactions with you. It is my duty to support the welfare of the unit assigned to the Tower, and I can't report what I don't observe. I'd welcome your input into how you feel you are being treated. Will that earn me my apology?"

Garik saw her differently. He glanced at Vang, who stood with his arms behind his back, his face blank and watching the wall above Garik's shoulder. It stood out to him that both Vang and Valladao were equally freckled, Vang with his light complexion and Cambodian eyes, and Valladao so clearly not Cambodian yet with similar coloring. It was an odd thing to notice, but it was none of his business.

"Master Sergeant," Garik offered, nodding once more.

"Now that's rude." She smiled, though. "Ma'am, or my name, if you don't mind. Or Sergeant Valladao. I prefer Megan unless commissioned officers are present."

"Thank you, Megan." Garik relaxed his guard. "I prefer Garik, and I apologize for thinking you were an Airman."

"An unintended slight, perfectly understandable from a civilian, and thank you. Shan tells me he's assigned to escort you to your quarters. Your supervisor is out of commission for a time—"

"Jailer," Garik muttered, glancing at Vang before looking to the floor. He was aware that he should shut up, but everyone always wanted him to shut up, and he was tired of shutting up. "That's his real job, and no one's bothered to tell me if he's still alive."

"Let's not say jailer. Or guard or bouncer or anything like that. It disrespects the man. I know Devon, and he likes working with the people here in the facility." She smiled briefly. "Do you have any complaints about him?"

"None, just that he needs to wear pajamas at night."

"Pajamas." Her eyes twinkled. "Noted. Anything else?'

"Can I see him? Another thing, I'm staying in his apartment, and I don't have a passkey."

"Shan?" She directed the question at the Airman.

"I have one here, ma'am." Vang pulled a passkey from inside a pocket, and he held it out. "It will allow *Garik* entry and egress to the apartment and permission to ride the elevator to the Level 1 cafeteria and the Level 4 hospital."

"And Level 3 for training," Valladao elaborated, revealing that she had known about the passkey and was allowing Vang a level of control and responsibility over Garik as his new jailer. "You will need to validate your thumbprint before using it. Shan will help you with that. Okay, we're here, and I'm good. Garik, feel free to contact me if you need anything. I'm sure Shan can accompany you to check on Devon, or if he feels you can be trusted . . ." She looked at Vang. The elevator dinged and the door opened as she finished speaking.

"Yes, ma'am. I've got this covered." Vang gave her a salute.

"Garik, I'm sure we'll speak again." She nodded and exited the elevator.

"Okay, to the hospital. Is that what you wish?"

Vang held his thumb over the Basement 4 icon.

"Please." Garik noticed the change in the man. A thicker veneer of respect. He hoped it lasted, although it would be weird if Vang started calling him by his first name. Garik absolutely didn't want to address the Airman by Shan.

He shivered at the thought of that.

THE VISIT to the hospital was informative but not as much as Garik had hoped. They learned Devon was indeed alive and out of surgery. His leg had required the most work and he would likely wear a cast for months. To visit? Not possible, not today, as he was fully saturated with painkillers. Inquire in a day or two, hopefully calling before visiting a second time.

Airman Vang returned with Garik to the main lobby in the tower to validate Garik's passkey. Charity Cellers wasn't at her desk, but Gunther Diehl was at the concierge's desk for Stamford Suites.

"Good morning, Airman Vang. And Garik, how nice to see you again. What can I do for the two of you today?" The concierge was cheerful and helpful, as always.

Vang explained the unvalidated passkey, and Gunther assured him he could help. He entered a code, Garik pressed his thumb to the passkey, and Gunther hit accept to link the passkey to Garik's identity. Garik mentioned to Vang that he hadn't eaten, so he accompanied Garik back to the elevator and to Level 1, and he continued on in the elevator, leaving Garik to find his way where he needed to go.

Garik headed to the cafeteria and was especially surprised to see Kevin Lee from Ai Kee! sitting at a table enjoying a meal with Bert Ellis and Jacquelien Van Kessel. Kevin's van was sandpaper in his memory. Garik had broken the window, and who knew what other damage it had taken when the Tower had stormed the parking garage under the Ransom Communications Building where Garik had parked it. And that was after Jantzen had assured the man he would take good care of it. Garik's enthusiasm for lunch soured, and he looked for an easy exit, but Bert had seen him and called to him, waving his hand.

Garik approached awkwardly, unsure of how to handle the van thing. It had been, what, only three days that Kevin had offered the use of his van? It seemed longer.

"Hello Bert, Jacquelien, Kevin." Garik ran a hand through his hair, unwilling to look Kevin in the eyes. "I'm sorry about your van."

"Yeah, about the van. You and Mr. Hefferly said, and I quote me, 'I know you'll take good care of the van, Mr. Hefferly,' and now I quote him, 'Of course, Kevin,' and now I don't have a job at the Center any-more. They didn't like their van coming back trashed."

"I'm so sorry." He really was. He hadn't meant for

Kevin to take the brunt of his poor decision to shatter the window when all he had to do was ask Giselle for the key. Now the Center had fired him. It was another black mark against everything he had become.

Kevin shrugged. "After the Hollywood shoot, I was too hot for them to handle. People coming by, getting in the way, all to see the movie star. Mr. Mandering said he wasn't running a celebrity show."

"But your autograph session at Chow Down. He was making money right and left." Garik slipped into a seat, his concerns about the van forgotten.

"He liked that." Kevin grinned. "He didn't like me giving them away for free at the Center. That's why I was giving Ms. Sunchaser private lessons here at the Tower. Hoping to go it on my own. Now, I am."

"But how did you get permission—" Garik cut off his question, unsure if he was allowed to even ask it. He looked to Jacquelien and Bert, searching for a lifeline. Jacquelien shrugged, and Bert grinned. "What? You guys, well, you look normal, but you know what happens down here. And they don't tell anyone. Much less city people."

"Hey, my man," Bert shifted position, and his black tattoos flexed under his net shirt like they were dancing, "this falls into my skill set. We all knew Kevin was teaching Halo, and when Devon took a fall, I matched up two and two, and Kevin made four." His eyes sparkled, and he looked at Jacquelien like it meant something special just between them.

"See," Kevin filled in, "I brought you up with Ms. Sunchaser after seeing you with Mr. Hefferly. Thought she might know something, you being deported back to Russia, then appearing in the Tower. Even I know that's not the way things happen. When someone's deported, they can't get back into the country, not without special reason. I think she wanted to buy me off with this job."

"Keep you close to keep an eye on you, more like it." The electrified sword in action. Garik tingled all over.

"Okay, fine, as long as I get a paycheck. She said I would be working with some enhanced people, and I would need to sign a confidentiality agreement. I said sure. So, my friend, are you enhanced, too?" He balled a fist and punched Garik on the shoulder. "If so, how?"

"Maybe. What about Callie? You were hot after her, as I remember." Callie Fornya worked at Ai Kee! and was the ex-Olympian poster girl for the franchise. Kevin had worshipped her, although she didn't seem to know he existed. Garik didn't want to talk about his "enhancements," and he was certain she would distract the man.

"Yah, it's been a while since you were around. Callie got married a few months back. Gonna have a baby. Not my thing."

"Who else have you met?" Garik glanced around

the cafeteria, which was mostly empty. "Do you have an apartment, yet? I mean, everyone down here has to, don't they?"

"Just us." Bert pointed to Jacquelien, Garik, and himself. "Not them." His hand shifted to Kevin.

"But Devon—" Garik hesitated. Surely they wouldn't give Kevin Devon's apartment. He liked Kevin and wouldn't mind him as a roommate, but the tablet under the couch. That was vital, and Kevin might ask questions Garik couldn't answer, not truthfully, anyway.

"Devon's choice." The red stripe on Jacquelien's face split when she opened her mouth to speak. "He could have lived in the Tower or anywhere in Bay City. He didn't have a reason to so stayed with the people he worked with. He liked us."

"Likes us, Jacke. He's not gone."

"Okay. Likes us. Bert wanted to be a welcoming committee, and I said, 'I'm open to anything.'" She laughed. "You can join us if you wish."

"Yes, please. Can I get something to eat, first? Breakfast was yesterday, and I haven't eaten since."

"I remember you and my nachos at Chow Down. You chowed down." Kevin teased. "I know where the food is. My first requirement when I accepted this job. I'll be right back."

Kevin stood and walked away, lithe and confident as a martial arts trainer should be. Garik whispered, "I know what you guys said, but Kevin being here shouldn't be possible. I'm glad and all, but what's the real reason?"

Bert glanced at Jacquelien. She nodded, and Bert leaned in. "You know why Devon was assigned you, don't you?"

"My jailer." He remembered Sergeant Valladao's remark about respecting the activities director and he took a deep breath. "Sorry, that was mean—"

"We understand." Jacquelien reached her hand as if to reassure Garik, then withdrew it before doing so.

"Since Kevin knows you—remember, he made the connection with Halo first—plus he promised to keep you, um, safe."

"Safe. Like, from what? And he doesn't live down here? How's he supposed to manage that?"

"That is the million-dollar question."

And it didn't get answered, because Kevin arrived with a steaming plate of nachos.

"Something I knew you would like," and he slipped the plate before Garik. He dropped several napkins and set a drink beside it.

Garik grinned and dug in, pleased for the moment, and willing to push his problems aside for a few minutes of taste-filled happiness.

— 8 —

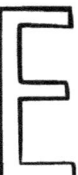

veryone knows there's a secret. Especially among the richies in the Tower. They just don't know what it is."

Bert and Jacquelien's tour was long over, and the idea of a game of racquetball had piqued Kevin's attention. Non-contact, the bloodline of the game, and a great way to get a workout, heh? Now, Kevin's hair was damp, and he gleamed with sweat.

"And you do?" Garik now did, and he wished he didn't. He swung, *whack*, and the ball hit the front wall, echoing with frustration and anger. Kevin leaped forward in response, missing the ball.

"Some of it, I guess, but likely not all. I know you. That was enough to get me interested." Kevin grinned. He pressed one shoulder to his face to clear perspiration from an eye. "You're quick. Don't you get tired?"

Tired of what, this? It was nothing compared to the secret. His girlfriend, Marisa, had been determined to ferret it out after her sister vanished into the Corona Tower cauldron of disappearing people, and it had swallowed him, toes, fingers, and ears.

And now, Kevin, stepping into it willingly. What was he thinking?

Kevin retrieved the ball and tossed it to Garik. He put his hands on his knees, his legs bent, breathing hard. Garik tossed the ball up, and *whack*, into the front wall. Kevin danced, returned the ball, and the game was in play.

Enough of an answer? Huh? Yet Garik was careful of one thing. Playing too well. When the rainbows shadowed the ball, his racquet, and Kevin; and the ball began to slow to easy speeds; he knew he was moving too fast. He also knew the consequences: exhaustion, complete and debilitating. He could go and go and go at a human level of endurance, but upping his play to that level of skill, whether it was competition or unfair DNA-enhanced mutant performance, took everything from him.

Better to play the game Kevin expected from him than the one he knew he could win.

"I'LL MAKE you a deal." Kevin stood before the mirror in the changing room, freshly showered and wearing street clothes. He put a comb through his hair, adjusting it to perfection.

"Hollywood style?" Garik was on a bench across the room, also freshly laundered, and tying his shoes. He looked up and watched in the mirror as the man grinned. Even from across the room, Garik's keen sense of smell revealed Kevin's tangy, fresh bodywash.

"You got me." Kevin flipped his comb to the counter and joined Garik on the bench, all energy and excitement. He put his elbows on his knees and leaned in like an old friend sharing a familiar story. "That was just for kicks. Boris wanted me to do that audition, but I knew it wasn't what I really wanted. I like the excitement, not the glamor."

"Boris with Lindemann Airways." Garik remembered him as a twenty-something richie with blue-tipped blond hair from one of the exclusive apartments in the Stamford Suites section of Corona Tower. His girlfriend was Kirsten Kaudlitz, an heir of the Kaudlitz hotel chain.

"Sure. He founded it, you know, the reason he has so many buckets of cash." Kevin rubbed his fingertips together like shuffling greenbacks. "I told you I had to sign a confidentiality agreement to work here. Right? I didn't tell you the rest."

"Okay." Garik didn't like this. Handcuffs, anyone? Locked doors? Was he about to lose his new passkey? What had Kevin agreed to that Garik wouldn't appreciate?

"It's like this." Kevin looked at the ceiling, pausing and tracing it with his eyes. "Is it private in here, I mean really private?"

"Probably." Garik recalled the microphone Devon had retrieved, the one secreted under a counter by Justin Kurtew. It wasn't likely the Tower had one. They promised privacy, or as much as possible, and Garik trusted them in that.

"Okay, then, all those demonstrations, that's me." Kevin sat back, and the electricity evaporated from him. He laughed a short bark of a sound. "Can you believe it? And Sunchaser hired me anyway."

"No handcuffs?" Garik held out his wrists, able to tease, finally.

"I don't get it."

"Jailer." The unintended word slipped out, breaking the crust of Garik's self-control, and his inner torment boiled out. "Isn't that why they hired you? You're the heavy, and I'm the mark? I was born in Russia. The police work for the politicians, not for the people. Don't tell me you weren't hired to rough me up if I don't follow the rules." *Shut up, Garik! My mind, my thoughts. Don't let out your anger. It never brings good things to you.*

"Hey, it's not like that. Well, I guess I did agree to some of that, but not like handcuffs or anything. I didn't agree to tie you to your bed at night, rather to, um, hang out with you. Yeah, that's right. How's that, hang-out buddy?" Kevin held up a fist, and he grinned. "Fist bump, buddy?"

"Okay, I give." Garik returned the fist bump. "Isn't hang-out old-person? My aunt says that, but I never do."

"Nah, I've always said it. Back to my story. I told you I asked Ms. Sunchaser about you, but here's what I didn't say, not with those guys out there." Kevin leaned in again. "Marisa knows something, that I've been sure of all along. About you, I mean. See, I asked her, and she acted like she didn't, like you had really been deported, but a guy can tell. Her eyes, her voice when I asked about you. I didn't believe any of it. Then when you showed up with Mr. Hefferly, well, what could that mean except that you were with Mr. Hefferly!"

"That doesn't make sense." Garik took to his feet, forced to move, thinking about Marisa, and remembering the last time he saw her, and how she had said she had missed him, too. It ripped him apart.

"But it does. Everyone knows Mr. Hefferly. His face is all over the adverts, the man who turns into purple mist. With a magic trick like that, how can you miss him?"

Magic trick. Kevin didn't know what he had signed

up for. At least Garik still had real ears, no tail, and hadn't begun howling at people yet. Maybe Kevin could continue in sublime ignorance a while longer. Wait until he met Justin, with wings and extra joints, more hybrid mutant than human hybrid. "So, what about Marisa?"

"She was the trigger. Like bang, when I saw you, I said, this is fishy. Boris' theories about something weird in the basements? Yah, something weird, so I decided to do something about it. The excitement over-rode my good sense, and there you go."

"I'm still not with you. Marisa and seeing me? How did that turn into weird things in the basement and demonstrations across Bay City?"

"No, no, not just that. I thought you knew about the footage on the news. You, on camera. Have you seen it?"

"Me falling on my face. I've seen it." Garik had made his way to the sink, and he looked at his face in the mirror. "Yeah. My friend showed it to me."

"Bam! You have lots of friends in the city. I should have so many." He looked sheepish. "Well, I guess I do, otherwise there wouldn't be such excellent crowds for all those demonstrations. Anyway, the next video was the big cannon."

"Next video?" Garik shifted his attention to Kevin's reflection, then he turned around. "What next video?"

"Them trying to silence you. Take you out. Prevent

you from ever talking about what's down here. It's part of me taking this job, except I need the money. That was important, too."

"Silence me?" And take him out? Was Kevin now also part of the looney toons? And Garik thought everyone in the Tower's basements had lost their minds. It had now spread everywhere.

"Here. You can't tell anyone I have this. It's all over social media." He pulled out a watch. "I recorded it before they took it down, and I sent it to everyone I know. I think it's from a surveillance camera from one of the fancy places along Park. Several people also uploaded footage, but this is the only one that shows the actual attempt on your life."

Garik tapped the image. The video title was *Merc vs. Truck, Truck Wins.* It played out in low-resolution black and white. Devon's little electric Mercedes appeared from one side of the picture, and then the massive military transport rumbled in from the other direction and dominated the image. He winced as the I-beam of a bumper attached to the military truck rolled over the small car like a can opener. He didn't see how anyone survived. He now understood why Devon was marinating in feel-good medicines and the confusion when Garik had shown no injuries at all at the hospital.

"You can access the Internet on this?" The video continued with people exiting the big truck and moving the small car off view before loading the victims into the large truck and continuing on as if nothing had happened. When it was played out, he offered the watch back to Kevin.

"Nah, locked up tight when I'm in here. But outside, sure. Why?"

"I want to know what's happening. Bert said you don't have to move down here full time. You can leave when you want."

"I can't take you, though, or tell anyone about you. Or anything else from down here. I did sign that agreement."

"Okay, let me think, then." He'd hoped he could get a message to his friends, but that didn't seem possible.

"They didn't say I couldn't tell you what I learn from out there, though." Kevin grinned.

"That's something." Garik sat beside Kevin, and he leaned back, his head against the wall, his eyes closed, trying to decide where to go. "You said you set up demonstrations. I watched a couple from the penthouse on the top floor. They've got Weston Rodheimer like a tornado looking for damage to do." Garik had never lived through a tornado, but he had seen Rodheimer threaten and cajole the human hybrids. The comparison was apt. "Tell me about them. And my face on that flag at the school. What do you know about that?"

Kevin laughed. "That's my favorite. But later. Here's what you can expect across the city. Sure, I can't participate now—"

"The agreement you signed." Garik waved off his disclaimer.

"Right, so you know I'm out of it. Hear that, microphones?"

"There aren't any." Garik kicked the side of Kevin's shoe with his.

"So you say, but I want the record clear, just in case. Here's what I did."

As Garik listened, he hoped his assurances about no microphones were accurate. If not, Kevin was likely to be strung up to dry. He'd scheduled repeated media posts, though that wasn't a real problem. Then he'd contacted several controversial fringe groups that liked to buck authority, a few of which had recently been embroiled with race issues and immigration policies.

"Race issues!" Garik snorted. "What race issues?"

"You're Russian, aren't you? That's a race, and that's the reason they said they deported you. Now we know they didn't, so that means they were lying. Why? And people already suspect something with so many people 'disappearing' into the Tower's workforce. Transferred overseas. No one believes that."

Garik had paid attention to the news before his induction. Current events had been a part of his high school classes. Fringe groups, especially radical ones, did bad things when they found a cause they could jump on. He wondered what bad things would happen to Bay City now that Kevin had them riled up.

He hoped Marisa wasn't involved.

And that flag with his face! That's what he wanted to know. Who had done that? C'mon, Kevin, get to the good stuff!

— 9 —

evin fell easily into his new position as the underground research center's recreation coordinator and activities director.

The human hybrids on the five floors of the basement complex needed direction in their training, schedules needed organized, and supplies and material had to be ordered and maintained in an accessible manner.

When Garik described Devon Maye's penchant for wearing an oversized fanny pack, Kevin at first thought he was teasing. When Garik brought out one and showed him how much it held, Kevin laughed and insisted he could come up with a less embarrassing solution. The less embarrassing solution was Garik, which was fine with him. He got to trail along with the championship-winning martial arts expert, and along the way, he discovered that martial arts was a much broader discipline than he expected.

"Of course, I don't just sit around and kick box all day." Kevin laughed. "I box, the real kind, and wrestle, and you played me at racquet ball. I nearly smashed you into the wall."

"Because I let you." Seriously, Garik thought. I had to slow down to keep from beating you too badly.

"T'shush. Even American football, the only kind, in my eyes. A football player is better if they wrestle or train in martial arts. I even swim. I was a diver in high school."

"Did you compete?"

"Not good enough. My strength was elsewhere, but I enjoyed it. Here, I get to do it all."

ONE AT a time, they met with the various people Kevin would begin training. Among them, Stephen Klandermans, narwhal bonded, was focused on gym-nastic skills. His super-dense bone structure allowed him to endure bone-jarring landings that would shatter other people. Kevin's job was to keep Stephen from shattering himself. The man didn't see his own limits and didn't like being told.

Ineke Van Stekelenburg, vastly strong from her ant DNA infusion, faced an uphill battle from her recent injury. Kevin suggested fencing. It would give her time to heal while learning control and developing lightness on her feet.

Jacquelien Van Kessel and Bert Ellis trained together. They were in the natatorium most days. Kevin and Garik joined them at the start of their sessions, but they were capable and motivated, and they didn't require supervision.

Garik described the training session he'd attended with Lansana Opoku-Mensah, and Kevin was intrigued. After a day's consultation with Lansana, they agreed that she didn't require speed to survive, but she would build a better disguise with finesse. So, she began ballet training. Small movements to create the impression of what she wanted others to see. Lansana took to it like second nature.

Paul Gberie needed group skills, interactive cooperation, to not stand on his own but to achieve a goal as part of a group. He needed team sports, and Kevin challenged him to choose between basketball and soccer. "Ah, sokker," Paul laughed. "True football. I have made my choice."

Benjamin Fuest had a recently injured femur and he said he must rest before he could even think of training. He would be glad to produce a medical exemption if Kevin wished. Kevin said he could revisit his training options later.

Veronika Abbink and Zekeria Salem wanted to combine a mix of speaking, presentation, acting, and standup comedy.

"That's training?" Kevin was surprised at the non-sports selections.

"They are our strengths." The two seemed pleased to have made their own choices.

"I have to show you're doing something, um, physical. Do you use the climbing wall, like, ever?"

"Do we, Veronika?" Zekeria raised his eyebrows at the woman.

"I'm sure we will now, Zekeria."

They laughed and turned to walk away. Kevin called after them, "Document your time on the wall. I'll look for it."

They waved over their shoulders and continued walking.

"People," Kevin moaned.

In between training sessions, preparing for training sessions, and stowing gear after training sessions, Garik learned bits and pieces of what was happening outside.

"So, what's happening today?" Often Garik's first question when Kevin arrived at breakfast.

"What happened last night, you mean. Today, I'm as clueless as you are." He tapped his watch. "No Internet means no news. I know what you know."

"Not true. You know way more than I do."

"What? Say that again."

"I said, you know way more . . . oh, I get it." Garik grinned, caught out.

"It's about time you admitted it." Kevin cut into pancakes with syrup and butter and forked a large slab into his mouth. "Who was your babysitter last night?"

"They locked me in my room."

Garik was still in Devon's apartment. His bed had been delivered Kevin's first day, and the new activities director had helped him rearrange the space and set it up. His ZBoard charger had already been moved, and even after his door was repaired, no one asked him to change back. His biggest disappointment was the tablet under the couch. He discovered it would allow him to preview incoming messages but remained locked to Devon's ID. With Devon in the hospital . . . well, it was as good as useless to Garik. At night, either one of the staff stayed in the apartment, or Garik was forced to stay with them. They could disengage his key function remotely, so he had no choice. Tag along or be stranded on his own. He felt like a stepchild being shunted between parents, none of whom wanted him.

"Humiliating, I know," Kevin commiserated.

"You could come live down here. You'd have your own room." Garik pleaded.

"I've seen where you live. No thanks. I like sun and sky. Besides, how else would I be able to keep you up on the outside news?"

Kevin was right. But for Garik, being watched over like an unwanted stepchild was demeaning, and he was ready for something to change.

"So, what happened last night?" Garik looked forward to the answer each morning. The stories were his version of knights in armor or of castles and dragons, and the audaciousness of the events Kevin relayed was every bit as exciting.

"A car was set on fire last night." Kevin seemed unconcerned as he licked one finger.

"In Bay City? Nah." Still, Garik lapped up the possibility. It was what he had left Russia to escape during the ethnic hostility his family had tried to shield him from. It was as exotic to him as the memory of his former home.

"I drove by it. I took a picture for you." He unclipped his watch, held it out, and there it was, red flames and black smoke. Wooden sticks and crumpled placards littered the ground, and people were cheering. Several were waving flags, one U.S. and another matching the one that had hung at the school.

"There's a flag of me!" The car no longer seemed the central theme of the image. Why was he on a flag in a picture of a burning car?

"Yikes!" Kevin took the watch, tapped it, and let out a hard sigh. "Wrong picture. I took a second one without that person. Here. Enjoy this version."

"No." Garik pushed the watch away. "You don't get

off that easily. Why am I on that flag?"

"Because you started this." Kevin pushed his plate back. "Rather, it all started *with* you. My apologies. *You* didn't start anything."

"Why were you trying to hide it? You've got to tell me." Garik rapped the table, his frustration close to boiling over.

"Not so loud." Kevin held up his hand and pressed the anger away. "It's getting bad in the city, more than I intended. The high school—"

"What about the high school?" Muhammad, Ibn, Hayat . . . and Marisa and Maria and Alexi. All the people he knew from school. Surely Alexi was out of detention. Then there were Giorgio and Robbie . . . and Wajeha, all of them. He wanted to hear everything.

"The school has been closed for three days. How do you like that? Everybody you know, placard carrying do-gooders all."

"How . . . why?"

"You really don't get this, do you?" Kevin took a deep breath. "The school is closed due to bomb threats. The police are guarding the water towers, and I've been bringing a change of clothes in case I can't get home at night."

"Yikes." Garik sat back, stunned. "I didn't know."

"Exactly the way the Tower wants it. I'm on your side, my friend, but I'm playing two games here. You can't share any of this down here. It would all come back to me."

"Got it." Garik lifted a hand to draw a finger across his lips to zip them closed when the lights overhead flickered once, then dimmed, then went out altogether, leaving them sitting in the gloom of near darkness. Small amounts of light filtered from the main lobby where skylights let in the outside world.

"O—kay." Kevin moved his chair, and in the darkness, the sound of the metal feet on the hard floor reverberated.

"It's never done this before." Garik pictured the elevators, poking in the passkeys and punching the buttons, and the elevators refusing to release them to the outside. On the floors below them, it would be worse. They had no skylights, except in Corona City, where the pool ceiling cut through Level 1 to a windowed skylight to mimic an outside environment. Everything else would be blacker than black, except for battery powered devices.

Then, Devon! If he were awake, he would be terrified. And it was all Garik's fault. If only he'd told him about the message from Dieter instead of hiding that he knew where the tablet was.

"Kevin, I want to check on Devon. Can we get to the hospital, do you think?"

"There's a power generator down here, right? I was told that, I think. How long before it kicks on?"

"I don't know. Can we?" The air began to move,

and with a flicker and a buzzing sound, the lights came on with an audible click. They were dimmer than before. "Now, can we?"

"Yeah, kid. Let's go get trapped on a lower floor. That's what you want, we'll do it."

"What's wrong?" Even Garik could see the man's color washed out.

"I told you. I need the sun. You said it's never done this before, right?"

"Not since I've been here." He watched the lights. Two minutes were about right for the backup generators, and they had to build to full power, meaning they weren't on city power.

"Okay, let's go get lost in the dark. I don't know if we're on city power or Tower power. Get it, kid? City power or Tower power? Either way, it's this way. Elevator, ho!"

Garik watched Kevin's eyes. They had never seemed so large. He didn't know adults could be as scared as he was. He wanted Kevin to be in control. If adults weren't, well, he didn't want to even think of that.

THE ELEVATOR worked fine. It was backed up with others who had arrived before them, and they had to wait for several minutes. However, Kevin's assigned passkey got them to the hospital level without incident. As they exited, the car filled up with people headed the other way, several with nursing staff in attendance.

"Okay, that was strange." Garik looked back. "They should be coming to the hospital, not leaving."

"Not the only strange thing." Kevin's mouth was tight. "Being down here is another."

The lights brightened as they moved along the ribbon candy walkway toward the hospital entrance. The people they met seemed preoccupied, and many of them kept glancing at the lights, as if unsure how long they would remain on.

At the main desk, confusion reigned. After a minute they got someone's attention and requested, "Devon Maye, please. Visitors."

"Maye, Maye, yes. He's not with us any longer."

"He died?" No! They had been in to see him only days before. Garik couldn't imagine it!

"Oh, no. No, of course not. You likely just missed him. We're moving non-emergencies. He's on his way to his apartment. Do you know where that is?"

"Yes," Garik said. "I live there."

"Then you don't need directions." The nurse turned and busied herself at other tasks.

Garik pictured Devon's cast and wondered how he could walk. Then, he realized he wasn't a stepchild any longer. His babysitter was back.

The ride on the elevator was all uphill to him.

— 10 —

ey, Devon, it's good to have you back." Garik burst into the apartment, pleased to see his friend on the couch and sitting up.

"Thanks." Devon attempted to stand, but one leg was wrapped in a full cast and propped up on the coffee table. "Hey, Kevin," he called, as he struggled to get up.

"Nah, I don't think so." Kevin stepped forward and pushed his shoulder. Devon sank back into the cushions. "No need to prove anything with us."

"So, if you're not well, why did they kick you out

of the hospital?" Garik dropped next to him, surprised at how much it meant to have him back.

"I hardly think I was kicked out." Devon knuckled Garik's knee and chuckled. "I suspect they expect I could get better care from you than from them."

"Have you lived with this guy?" Kevin snorted. "He barely knows how to change his own socks."

"Yeah, I know. Typical teen. Still, I've missed you, kiddo. Good to be together again, right-o?" Devon winked at him.

"Right-o, Devon-o." Garik grinned. "What can I get for you?"

"News. What's going on up there?" He thumbed toward the ceiling. "I know nothing, except that the power went down, and the hospital said they would be short-staffed for the day. If we were ambulatory, we were out of there. Do I look ambulatory to you?"

"I hope looks are deceiving," Kevin said.

"Look what I found." Garik reached under the couch and brought out the MicroArt tablet. Revealing it was a pit in his stomach. "I'm sorry you didn't have it and missed Dieter's text."

"Not your fault, kiddo, but I'm glad to have it back." He took it and fell into it, immediately typing inquiries and notifications. Moments later, he spoke to Kevin. "You changed everyone's schedule. How's that working out for you?"

"For me? Busy. For everyone I'm working with,

great, I think. The kid's been with me every day. Incredibly useful. Couldn't have done it without him."

"You, the pride of the team." Devon wrapped a hand around Garik's knee and dug in with his fingers. Then he punched him on the shoulder. "If you want to be useful this morning, how about you get me some coffee. You know how to make that?"

"Sure. Kevin's taught me." The dread of revealing Devon's missing tablet dissipated with the request.

"Right-o. He's a good man. So, go."

GARIK HAD *watched* Kevin make coffee, so his assurance to Devon was more hopeful than accurate. He did know what the coffee maker looked like and where it was located.

He enjoyed listening to his two mentors talking—no longer jailers, not with Devon back—sharing the traits of each person on the training schedule and discussing the possible repercussions of the power failure. The location of the coffee threw him off, until Kevin caught his eye and pointed up. He located it in an upper cupboard, relieved. He opened the package and pulled out a scoop and panicked. He looked back to Kevin who held up two fingers, and Garik dipped them out and poured them inside. He added water and turned it on before returning to the board meeting in the living room.

Devon had been accessing his tablet, looking up from time to time, laughing, or asking questions of

Kevin, when something on the tablet seemed to grab his attention.

"Kevin, um, you're still in your apartment in the city, right?"

"Absolutely. Why?"

"Then you are keeping track of what's going on up there. The, um, stuff that's happening?"

"Let me see that." He took the tablet and scrolled through several images. "Some of this I haven't seen, but yes. There's the one I showed you this morning."

He handed it to Garik, and Devon intercepted it before Garik could take it. Still, Garik had seen it, and he moaned, "That flag. People, what's with the flag?"

"He's seen this?" Devon seemed surprised. "Tell me you didn't show him."

"Well," and Kevin shrugged. "If you want the truth . . ."

"Aren't you, I mean, you did sign the agreement, didn't you?" almost like it was a secret Garik couldn't be told.

"Oh, that." Kevin grinned. "I took it like this: I can't give out any information about the research facility, but there was nothing in there that said I had to shield this place from the outside. Besides, your boy pumps me every morning for information. How can I resist?"

"So, what has Kevin told you?" Devon glanced at his tablet, studying the screen.

"Everything, I think." He looked at Kevin, who nodded. "I don't know why the power went out, but Kevin can't access the Net in here, so he won't be able to tell me until in the morning. Other stuff, yeah, like the bomb threats at the high school. They haven't had classes for three days."

"So, Kevin's our leak." Devon seemed to come to a decision. "I have more current information, thanks to my tablet. It links to my router which can access the outside Net directly. Look at this."

He held out the tablet, and on the screen, a current news article boasted, "Social Media Fuels Continued Blackout in Bay City."

"The Director said he wanted to eliminate all social media in Bay City, but he can't." Garik reached for the device to read more.

"One more thing." Before he handed it over, Devon turned it around and scrolled. This time, a video played, melting Garik's morning.

"That's . . . not possible." A crowd gathered around a large power company circuit breaker the size of a tractor-trailer rig. A large military truck, likely stolen, had been turned loose to crash into it. The front of the truck was blackened and foamed with flame retardant. The cheering crowd held a mix of flags and placards, some of which showed Garik's picture, and others saying, "Free the Boy," or, "Where's Garik?" Among them were people Garik recognized from Bay City High, although none of his closest friends. Words scrolled across the bottom of the screen. *Will the shipping docks be next? Corona Tower needs to respond before more damage occurs.*

"Respond to what?" Garik fought his face for self-control. He didn't want to be the catalyst for revolution in Bay City. He would sure enough be deported.

"It's happening again." Kevin twirled one finger in a circle at his temple. "Sheesh, to use Garik's word."

"What? What's happening again?" *Tell me,* Garik thought.

"Always. I've seen it numerous times." Devon retrieved the tablet and nodded with a grin.

"What? Just tell me!" Garik wailed. He wanted to strike out. He wasn't a kid, and he deserved to know.

"Chill, kiddo. We're on your side. You, repeating the obvious." Devon looked to Kevin. "Should I clue him in, or do you want to?"

"I will. That car that burned. Remember?"

"Sure." Garik clinched and unclenched his fists.

"And those videos of you?"

"Just tell me."

"I am telling you. People know you're here, more than I've let on. Someone out there is on your side, and they are getting the word out. You, my friend, are stirring up Bay City, and the muck is going everywhere."

"I'll be deported." Garik fell into a chair, consumed with the news. "I just want to be left alone."

"Well, for one, I think the excitement is fantastic. It's the reason I skipped Hollywood. This is the best thing that's happened to me since I won nationals." Kevin grinned.

"Better than Callie?" Garik was glad he could at least tease.

"Oh, much better, especially since she's having a kid now. Not mine, by the way."

"Callie?" Devon frowned. "Okay, kiddo, what have you guys been keeping from me? I want to know all about Callie."

"Sure." Kevin dropped into the chair across from Devon and leaned forward, sharing the story of the failed Olympic competitor.

Garik watched them talk, his own world closing in on him. *Getting the word out.* Who? Muhammad? Ibn? Or maybe Dieter with the rich father and an apartment in Stamford Suites?

He wanted Marisa on his side, but the last time he'd contacted her, the Tower had slammed him back into their basement dungeon. He glanced at Devon's tablet, once more wishing he could contact his friends. He wanted to know more, and he suspected he wasn't hearing everything.

Especially about the people he cared about. That was what he needed most.

THE COFFEE pot dinged, and Garik was startled back

to the present. He stood, and the two men barely registered his movement. The aroma of the coffee permeated the room, either that or it seemed that way to Garik because his sense of smell was so acute.

As he poured the coffee into two cups, the lights flickered and brightened. Garik watched to see if they remained on.

"City power." Devon studied the lights in the ceiling. "It's done this before, just not in a while. This is definitely city power. Let me see what I can uncover."

He fell back into the tablet, and Kevin moved toward the kitchen for his coffee. His watch dinged.

"Hm. That's strange. Why is this notifying me now?" He looked at it like a foreign object he'd never seen. He tapped it and nodded. "My morning session with Paul. We're assigning volunteers for possible soccer teams, and I need to be there. Devon, are you okay with Garik staying here? There's nothing for him to do except watch us talk. No game time today."

"More, I *need* him to stay. I've got this." He tapped the cast that had him tied to one spot on the sofa. "You good with that, kiddo?"

"Right-o." Garik found it easy to fall back into the familiar teasing banter.

Kevin left at a run, and Garik carried one of the cups of coffee to Devon. "Anything in it?"

"I'm a black man. You want Kevin's cup?" He nodded toward the counter.

"I can try it, if you think I should."

Devon shrugged. "Your call. You can add sugar to sweeten it or pour it back. It'll keep in the pot."

"Don't think there is any sugar." He didn't move to empty the cup. "It's good to have you back."

"You told me." Devon chuckled. "But thanks."

"I'm sorry about the tablet."

"Why? You found it. What's there to be sorry about?"

"The wreck. You were in a hurry. That was my fault."

"Okay, explain." Devon laid the tablet beside him, just about where it had been when Garik had first found it.

"I knew where it was that first day. It received a message, and I thought I could access the outside Internet with it, and I didn't want you to take it away." Garik's voice choked, and his eyes burned. "I really messed up, didn't I?"

"Maybe, but heh, kiddo, I was driving. You didn't have that accident. I did. But since you brought it up, about my car. I didn't hear how badly it was damaged. Have you seen it since the accident?"

"Yeah. I don't guess you saw the clip." Garik sniffled and wiped at his eyes before moving to sit beside Devon. "Kevin showed me. The Tower tried to take it down, but Kevin saved it before they did and sent it to everyone he knows. Search for *Merc vs.*

Truck. I bet you'll find it."

It was in there a few layers deep but not difficult for Devon. He watched the entire thing and pointed to the driver that exited the big truck.

"You know who that is, don't you? Your favorite person."

"Airman Han. I talked to him that night."

"You talked to him?" Devon clicked to replay the video, stopping and stepping it forward when the little car began to roll under the big truck's bumper. Looking closely, they could see the occupants flailing around as the car was crushed, at one point setting off several air-bags. "And how are you not in the same condition as me?"

"I heal pretty fast."

"Oh, you do?" Devon grabbed his neck and, with the other hand, ground his knuckles into Garik's scalp.

"Sorry." Garik laughed. "I'll try to heal slower next time."

"You didn't tell, did you?" Devon rubbed harder.

"No, no, stop!" Garik pulled away, panting with laughter. "Jantzen says never give everything away. I said it was your blood."

"Good. He's a smart man. Now, kiddo, another cup of coffee, please."

"Sure, big kiddo. Anything you want." And Garik meant it.

ccasionally, Garik stayed with Devon on the days when his leg bothered him too much to maneuver on his own. Most days, however, the dark-haired teen was with Kevin in the recreation area or locked in one of the soundproof training cells, quizzing the various hybrids for any information he could get from them.

He was desperate to know that his own induction into the human-hybrid project was, if not a total success, not a failure. He had traded his city life, his friends, and possibly his future for what had amounted to little of nothing. Better hearing, he could run fast, and he healed quickly. Worth it? He had yet to think so.

Outside news filtered in through Devon's tablet and from Kevin's evenings and weekends. The tablet forecasted the anger seething in the city. Kevin revealed the individual downdrafts that buffeted the Tower's authority and power at every turn.

The first citywide power disruption had only lasted several hours, the first harbinger of the coming storm. Several others were longer, with Old Town going dark at one point for nearly two days. The Tower was unaffected, likely because they now kept their in-house power plant online and fully operational at a moment's notice. The lights would flicker, and things would go on as normal, if at a slightly reduced level of brightness.

Devon hadn't offered Garik his outside access password to his computer, telling him he was willing to share what he learned on his tablet, but only because Garik would learn it all from Kevin anyway. To let the teen explore the real-world Net on his own? Not if he had control over it.

Kevin's arrival each day was a boon for Garik.

"Good morning, people." Kevin had taken to showing up at Devon's apartment in Corona City. Today, he seemed more harried than usual.

"Who are we training today?" Garik had come to enjoy Kevin's sessions with the modified humans in the secretive basement complex. Learning what they could do and seeing them in action was better than any video game he had ever played.

"Soccer game." Kevin mimed kicking a pass with the inside of his foot.

"I knew today would be Paul!" And lots of people Garik didn't know, including non-hybrids from other departments in the research complex: medical, staffing, and office workers, all signed up in the new soccer league. Even Tyrone had joined them in their last game.

"Before you two head off to kick balls with Paul and whoever else joins the game, let's have breakfast." Devon had crutches leaning against the arm of the couch, with foam swim noodles—provided by Kevin—cut and fastened to the top part of each crutch. He shifted his cast off its cushion on the top of the coffee table and leaned for the crutches.

"I can prepare breakfast." Kevin dropped his things on the table, to be stopped by Devon.

"No. I need the exercise. I'm turning into jello. Me getting up is good for everyone, me especially. I might go berserker on you guys."

"Can't have that." Kevin grinned at Garik.

"And Annie is in town and stopping by to see me." Annie was Annie Vanschooneveld, the Tower's foreign affairs attaché. She traveled most of the month, but she had a thing for Devon and hadn't been in town since his accident. Devon seemed pleased.

"Ah, the truth. You need to shave and put on clean clothes."

"That, too." Devon tugged on his crutches to get up, and he hobbled to the kitchen. On the way, he dropped his tablet in front of Kevin. "Tell me what you know about that."

"Can I look?" Garik leaned forward, doing his best to catch a glimpse.

The tablet showed a section of streets between First and Ninth. Garik recognized Stanners Tower at Eighth and Elm in the background. Cars barricaded intersections, tents were set up in the streets, and people gathered in layers of clothing around makeshift fires.

"That's near my house," Garik exclaimed. His aunt's house, actually, six blocks away, but close enough. "What are they doing?"

"It's called Take the City. They've named it the Tower Free Zone. Birch to Cherrywood, the entire section between First and Ninth. You can see the barricades they've set up. Electric fences in some places. You have to sign a document that you are a free person and don't owe allegiance to Corona Tower or Bay City before they'll let you enter."

"First and Ninth blocked off?" Devon leaned hard on his crutches and rubbed his head. The injuries to his temple were scabbed over, and he scratched at one before dropping his hand.

"You can still drive First and Ninth, just nowhere in between."

"I used to go to We Got Junk." Garik studied the

image, remembering. "Do you know Wesji there?"

"Sorry," Kevin said. "I do know they've posted signs at the barricades. I've driven by. You can see them easily along First and Ninth."

"Let me see it." Devon held out his hand, and he scrolled to see more. "That's Central Park. Are those homeless people?" Tents and accumulated trash gave a rag-tag appearance to the once pristine grounds.

"There's been a call out on social media for people to join in the revolt—"

"We're revolting, now?" Devon shook his head. "What next, military intervention?"

Garik recalled the video posted about his recapture by the Tower's security forces. The military was already involved.

"According to social media, it is a revolt. People are being bussed in from Nevada and Oregon to join the cause." Kevin rubbed his neck. "I wasn't sure I could get here today with the crowds. And everything that happens, someone snaps a picture and uploads it. Then it's shared over and over."

"Can I search?" Garik was never given the tablet, and the computer in the apartment had him locked out of the outside world.

"Sorry, kiddo." Devon glared at Kevin. "Tell me what you want, and I'll do the searching."

Kevin encouraged him. "You'll find pics of my car entering the parking garage."

"I've seen them." Devon was to the kitchen, and he pulled milk from the fridge with eggs and cereal. He was working one-handed, and it looked precarious, but he hadn't dropped anything yet.

"Messages. Are you looking at any of that? And not just pictures." Perhaps Garik's friends—

"Accounts? If you know any logins, I'll be happy to see if they are saying anything." Kevin held a hand over the tablet, ready to type.

"Careful what you offer," Devon warned. He dropped butter in a pan, and it sizzled.

"It's okay. Go, kid. I'm ready."

Garik threw out his favorite social media sites, several of which he knew didn't need logins, not unless you wanted to post. He had to specify accounts, and he named places, businesses, and people he knew. It surprised him that the Tower had accounts, also. He was fascinated to find what they had to say.

CORONA TOWER'S social media accounts painted blue skies and good weather, including two-night specials at Stamford Suites and a discount code for Chow Down. They also offered parking garage vouchers with receipts from The Luncheon Lady. Even the movie schedule at the Tower's 10-Plex was online for everyone to see.

"What?" Garik was crushed. "They have discount codes for Chow Down? Why hasn't anyone told me before?"

"Do you visit their website or their social media pages?"

"Well, no." Still, he thought, he'd paid more than he had to, and that wasn't fair.

"Okay, then, don't complain." From the kitchen, Devon grinned.

Kevin continued to explore, and sometimes, posts let them link to accounts of places and people Garik didn't know. They followed the links, gathering information. The images of signs posted around the city and graffiti on city buildings were telling, but Garik wanted to see texts from people. Marisa, Muhammad, and Ibn, to name a few. Irina, his aunt, didn't have a mobile phone, so he would have been surprised to see anything from her, but the others? They were online all the time.

Devon had managed breakfast passably well, with one leg, two crutches, and a cast that ran from his thigh to his foot. He called to the other two, set out plates and the food, and asked them to take what they wanted. He wasn't serving, so they needed to come and get it. He wanted to lie down before Annie arrived, so he would let them get on with their day. Leaning hard into the crutches, he lurched toward his bedroom, and once inside, he fell onto the bed, calling out, "I'm fine, if anyone asks. Just don't ask right now, cause I'm not willing to be polite if I have to answer."

"Okay, we won't ask," Kevin called with a laugh.

He pulled off his watch and held it in his hands. "I don't know if you should see this, and I don't want Devon to know."

"What?" If he couldn't tell Devon, then he wanted for sure to see it.

"Are you certain you want to? Once you see it, you can't take it back."

"That's not fair." Garik threw himself back in his chair and crossed his arms. "That makes me want to see it, and you know it. And you're telling me I might wish I hadn't. How can I know until I've seen it?"

"Just giving you the chance, you know, to back out. Now you can't say I didn't warn you. I found this series of pics on one of my feeds. I think you know some of the people."

The images were from a party. He looked at Kevin, "This is in the Tower, isn't it? Stamford Suites. We were there—"

"The day you disappeared. I thought you might recognize it. Flip through the pictures. You might recognize more than just the location."

He swiped, and there were three people laughing, and one was looking up, almost at the camera. Garik grinned. "That's Ibn." His familiar beard, almost full along his jawline, and a shirt that shouted out, Jezebel and the Sticks. His hair was in long dreads, gathered around him like a wreathing mass of snakes.

"Go on. You'll see more."

Garik did, and in another picture, in a kitchen this time, he recognized Dieter, the new boy whose father had built him the indoor skatepark. This had to be Dieter's apartment. He looked up at Kevin, who nodded and motioned with his hand for him to continue.

He was certain he saw the back of Hayat al-Haber's head, a headscarf tied with a rope. Who else would wear that in Bay City? It had to be his friend. He smiled at his friend's habit of saying, "What, what?"

There were people he didn't know, but Vladimir with his wrestler's shoulders and Giorgio wearing shoes that could only be in the current fashion were sitting knee to knee, deep in each other's eyes. Vladimir was grinning, and Garik could almost hear the joke.

"Why wouldn't I want to see this?" Garik had fallen into the images, and he didn't want to come back out. It was like he was there. He knew each person, and he could imagine exactly what they were saying and how they felt about each other. Even Robbie Icardi, but not with Wajeha. Robbie held a bowl of chips and seemed to have claimed them as his private fiefdom. Then, Robbie was fifteen—or had been fifteen when Garik was inducted—and had no business with a serious girl-friend, anyway.

"You must have missed one." Kevin took the watch and scrolled back. "There. I saved it somewhere else. Here." He handed the watch back.

Garik's heart was gutted. In happiness, in pain, in

longing, he couldn't say. It was Marisa, it had to be, though he couldn't clearly see her face. Still, her hand was at her temple, obscuring her cheek, and shifting her dark hair away from her face, just the way Marisa would do. She was alone, looking out an expansive window, and she seemed filled with longing for something outside. Garik followed her view, and like an arrow, he took in the drone aircraft trailed by a long banner filled with words.

THEY ARE FEEDING US LIES. TAKE BACK BAY CITY TODAY.

"Notice her shirt."

Garik realized it was the picture of him he had seen on the school flagpole. He flipped through the images, faster and faster, occasionally stopping to study one. He looked up. "Except for Ibn's, they're all of me."

"You think they know?" Kevin grinned. "Okay, I have a session, and you're with me. Now. Hustle."

Garik did. No more did they step outside, than they ran dead smack into the biggest man in Corona Tower.

"Mr. Lee. I see you have your protégé with you. Good. And you, Garik, are just the person I was looking for. Come with me."

Garik sagged. His good day, foiled once again.

our supervision is unnecessary today, Mr. Lee. I am responsible for Mr. Shayk for the time being. I will either return him to Mr. Maye or notify you of my need for your continued assistance." Weston Rodheimer smiled, but his use of last names spoke more than his measured manner and even tone suggested. Two uniforms behind him didn't bother to smile.

"Thank you, Mr. Rodheimer." Kevin nodded. "Is everything okay?"

"In good time. I believe you are due to oversee a soccer game. Halo has been monitoring your work with us. She approves, and so do I. I am surprised to see you were able to get through this morning. Commendable. Now, if you will excuse us." With a nod, the Director dismissed the smaller man.

Garik watched Kevin walk away, trying to read the undercurrents between them. Whatever wasn't being said was out of his depth, and he knew he might as well let it go. As a woman at the next junction in the corridor walked past, paying them no mind, the Director's expression darkened, and his shoulders shifted under his clothing. The transformation was that of a fighter in a ring dominating an opponent.

Garik felt dominated, and he wondered what game they were about to play. He doubted he would understand the rules or that Rodheimer would choose to share them with him if he asked.

"Now, boy, we have matters to attend to. Follow me." Rodheimer turned, surprisingly light on his feet for his massive girth, and headed toward the elevators. The two heavies fell in behind Garik, and there was nothing to do except try to keep up.

"TELL ME what you see, Mr. Shayk."

They had entered a security monitoring station unfamiliar to Garik, an amphitheater lined with massive screens stacked five high and thirty or more side to side. About half showed corridors, likely somewhere in the research facility, and in several, people walked past, about their business. He found Kevin's soccer game in progress just as the ball was put into play. Another showed a hospital operating theater, although Garik didn't know enough to tell the procedure being done.

A handful of the screens were dark, and one winked out as they watched. The rest revealed chaotic views of the city. He recognized the mall, the interior of the parking garage looking out towards Stamford Drive, and a view overlooking Central Park. The tents and littered grounds were the same as on Devon's tablet, just from a different angle. Other views revealed people running, wrecked cars, and suited goons in black riot helmets. One of the black goons threw something, and smoke billowed out.

"Is that tear gas?" In Bay City? Even Garik knew this was bad if they were using tear gas. That only happened in third world countries, and well, his native Russia when people didn't behave as the government wanted.

"Likely. We are under siege. Do you understand that word?"

"Like a castle." He might be a teenager, but he wasn't stupid—or uneducated. Sheesh!

"Without a moat, but to use your example, yes, like a castle."

"Raise the wall." Garik had been on the outside so many times when the twelve-foot-tall wall was raised during mall events to separate the city riffraff from the

Tower richies. He guessed Rodheimer had never been forced to stand outside and wish he were inside.

The Director chuckled. "Each time I begin to doubt you, you renew my faith in what you might become. This is bigger than the wall. Your influence has spread to the entire city. I have twice seen you act in a way that suggests you can help us now, if you wish."

"How can I help with this?" Garik felt the anger. His influence? Like he had started this? He was the victim.

"You play your cards close to your chest, as always." Rodheimer motioned, and a tablet appeared. He took it and held it to Garik. "Remember this?"

The video recording of his battle with Justin Kurtew. Justin was fast, spinning his knives into a blur, at one point striking Garik's arm. Blood spurted, then Garik was no longer there; rather, he was across the ring, and he held his arms around Justin, restraining him. Garik remembered Justin's slicing strike down his right arm, getting angry, and standing in shock for a moment before moving against his opponent. Yet, in the video, he was one place and then the next with no movement in between.

"And the table. You rescued the glasses. As if you could see what was about to happen before it took place."

The table. Rodheimer had smashed his hand down, splitting the tabletop, and Garik had stepped up his speed to keep their drinks from crashing onto the floor. He now wished he had let them shatter and bleed their contents out.

"Precognition. You know the term." Rodheimer retrieved the tablet and handed it off to an aide. "I am sure we've achieved our goal in you. Tell me, what about the destruction you see all around us? How have you brought this about? What else are you able to do that we don't know about?"

"I—" Garik had no words. He had known some of this through Devon's searches and Kevin's stories, but seeing it all at once overwhelmed him. But, he had done this? How? What skills had he developed that would allow him to turn Bay City upside down? Jantzen Hefferly could turn into purple smoke. Justin, with his newly developed wings, able to fly. Alyna Lindberg with her razor-sharp claws. They were out there, escaped, free to wreak all the havoc they wanted on the city. The one person that couldn't was him, Garik, the only human hybrid they had recaptured. They couldn't lay the blame for everything on those screens on him.

"Come, now. You can surely give us more than one word. Bay City is your home. I'm sure you want to preserve all the places you love. And the people. Your aunt, your girlfriend." He called out to no one in particular, "Avenue C and Sycamore," and one of the screens shifted to show The Flower Shop. Traffic still flowed along Sycamore, unobstructed, with no sign of the destruction from the other video feeds swirling across the mass of screens. White flecks floated in the air—snow, Garik realized—and the lights in the shop showed through the windows.

"What do you want?" Garik knew what the image was. A threat. He didn't know if Rodheimer would jettison the Bruni's flower shop with a military-sourced missile, shut it down with invented city code violations, or plow it under by widening the intersection and claiming it by right of eminent domain. Likely a missile, as the rest would be too slow to make an impact on Garik's participation today.

"This to stop. You are key."

"How am I key?" Garik's frustration spewed from him. He wanted to strike out, and he watched the room take on a rainbow-hued tint before backing down and regaining self-control.

Before Rodheimer could answer, the door burst open, and Colonel William Brace, with his firm step and straight back, strode in. He was followed by Major Alfred Lipstitch and Lieutenant Colonel Marjorie Fair.

"Colonel." Rodheimer frowned, but he acknowledged the man civilly. "Your presence is not necessary. We have this situation under control."

"As I see, Director." Brace let his eyes rove over the screens. "Absolutely under control, each atrocity on those screens."

"Yes," Rodheimer replied. "We have mobilized

security, and soon—"

"Are you a horse's behind, Director, or just so blind you wish to see only what you wish to see?" Lipstitch and Fair glanced away, pointedly giving Brace plenty of room to run. "The U.S. government has given you loose reins, and you have assured us our investment would yield the results we desired. Now, you are allowing bedlam to risk everything."

"Not allowing, Colonel." Rodheimer's words were tighter, and his eyes narrowed.

On one of the screens, a protester under a flag with Garik's picture on it tossed a glass bottle at a parked car. The bottle burst, and flames erupted over the vehicle, sending black smoke barreling skyward. In the scene, a youth with dreadlocks cheered, and Garik thought of Ibn. He wanted to know that his friends were safe, not if the Tower was under attack, or if the military's investments were "yielding the results we desired."

Another screen showed a protester hefting a broken brick. He looked into the camera feeding the image into the Tower's basement security room, and giving the camera an insulting hand sign, he lobbed the brick. It grew larger and larger, then the image on the screen became static and died.

The lights overhead flickered, the screens on the wall blanked for a moment before the images returned, and a second later, the room shivered.

"That was?" Lipstitch voiced the question.

The screen with the view of the aboveground parking garage looking out to Stamford Drive gave them the answer. Dirt and grit floated in the air, the brick and mortar making up the walls of the parking garage began to collapse inward, and as dust filled the air and occluded the camera's view, the screen went dark.

"Lockdown," Rodheimer barked. "Full alert. Walls up. Mobilize everything to clear that garage." He turned to Garik. "Okay, Mr. Shayk. The moat's in place. Tell me that you didn't see this coming, because I believe you did. You could have helped us avoid this disaster."

Rodheimer spun on his heels, walked past the military higher-ups without recognizing their presence, and exited just as red lights in the ceiling began flashing and an alarm wailed.

Garik watched the screens. He knew castles and moats and sieges. He knew how the wars were won. The people inside starved to death, either that or they began cooking and eating one another to stay alive. He didn't want to be eaten, not in stew or any other way.

He had to find a way to fix this, whatever that might take. Except, he had no idea where to begin.

In Book Six, the military makes its presence known in Bay City.

Taking the Tower
Book Six
The Human-Hybrid Project

Garik Shayk's induction and involvement in the Corona Tower's Human-Hybrid Project has destabilized Bay City. Fires burn in storefronts, and the Harbor Shipyards traffic is being obstructed.

The riots brought about by the Tower's cloaked secrecy and repeated refusal to tell the truth threaten to devastate the project and the military's substantial involvement. Under the guise of quelling civil unrest, the military flexes its muscle to step in and assume control of Corona Tower and the vital Human-Hybrid Project.

Can Garik use the situation to his advantage to make his escape from the Tower a second time?

The Human-Hybrid Project

Addictive!

A 10-book series you won't be able to forget. Explore each upcoming book, the characters, and more at www.thehumanhybridproject.com.

Book 1   Book 2

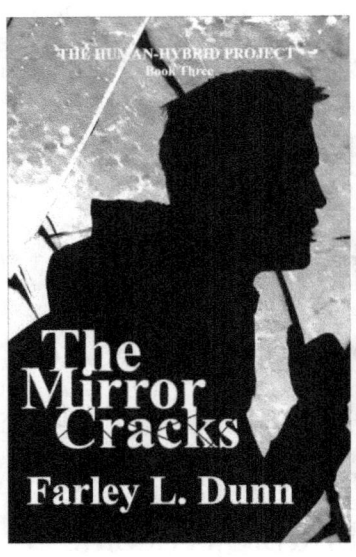

Book 3

Book 4

Book 5

Book 6

Book 7

Book 8

Book 9

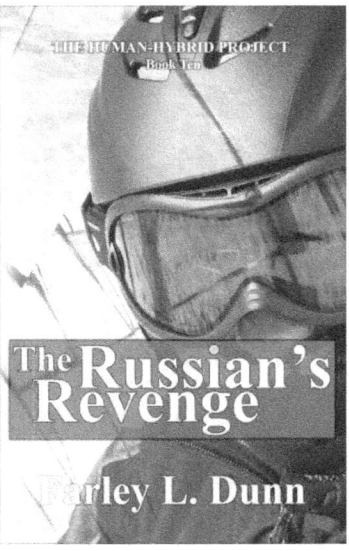

Book 10